Tobias Schmit, Auditor for the Supernatural Copyright © 2019
Steven L. Stamm

All rights reserved. No part of this book may be reproduced in any form or by any electronic or mechanical means, including information storage and retrieval systems, without written permission from the author, except in the case of a reviewer, who may quote brief passages embodied in critical articles or in a review.

This is a work of fiction. Names, characters, places, and incidents either are the product of the author's imagination or are used fictitiously, and any resemblance to actual persons, living or dead, events, or locales is entirely coincidental.

Published by **Kindle Direct Publishing**
Edited by **Jana Stamm & J. Walton**
Cover Art by Steven L. Stamm

ISBN: 9781798687413

The first year on the job is always the hardest.
   - *Trollum*

AUTHORS LETTER

Dear Reader,

It's all a joke. Remember that while you read this. Sometimes the joke will make you laugh till you cry and sometimes it will be in bad taste. Sometimes it is chaste and virginal and other times it is filthier than a cowboy's boots. That is the nature of true humor, and if you have picked up this book to read (and hopefully not to burn it) you must accept that. Also, after writing the short story "A bellhops guide to corpse disposal" I was asked why I make the font bigger than most other writers. I do this for two reasons. First, because I have a personal connection to people who have extreme issues with their eyesight. So, when designing my book I decided that everyone I love would be able to read it. Secondly because it makes the book have more pages and look more impressive, so it's a bit of an ego thing. And that is why for all my books the font size will always be larger than other people's.

Anyways, I hope you enjoy!

Signed

(Steven L. Stamm)

Tobias Schmit, Auditor for the Supernatural

"First year on the job"

KDP
www.Amazon.com

Name: Petyr Checkofsky
Location: New York City
Crime: Fradulent Insurance Claim and Orphan Arson, and appearing in books illegally.
Detained by
Agent Tobias W. Schmit

Current & Previous Work

' I laughed until I peed myself!'
R. O'connell, The Perpetually Perplexing Tales

'As bloody and brutal as it is funny!'
S. Castonella, A Bellhops Guide to Corpse Disposal

'If you want to be offended AND still be able to laugh. Look

no further'
M. Dwyer, Tobias Schmit Sampler

Name: The River Dragon Ti-Lee
Location: Louisiana
Crime: Murdered IRS Agent Thomason.

Detained by
Agent Tobias W. Schmit

Dedication

To my beloved wife
Thanks for putting up with me
I love you.

Name: Dragon Dog
Location: Arizona
Crime: Ate 295.5 Goverment Owned Livestock

Shot by
Agent Tobias W. Schmit

Acknowledgments

My wife

My friends, who encouraged me the whole way

My Readers who said my work was better than all the other losers.

Name: Duke Azeliphel of Hell
Location: Orlando Florida
Crime: Fradulent W-40 Form Submission

Fined by
Agent Tobias W. Schmit

Short stories by *Steven L. Stamm*

Story Titles:

The Perpetually Perplexing Tales

A Bellhops Guide to Corpse Dispoal

Prologue

"Two things are certain in this life, Death, and Taxes."
-Benjamin Franklin

"I don't give a farthing how much I owe, YOU CAN'T CHARGE ME INTEREST FOR ONE BEER!"
-Also Benjamin Franklin

"CRAP!", Natalie yelled loudly as she stumbled forward and started to fall for the third time that day. With practiced ease, she twisted herself into her fall. Skillfully falling onto her rear rather than her face. She sat sulkily on the floor and reflected on how she truly hated high heels with a deep burning passion, almost as much as she hated low-carb diets. But, her boss had insisted that if she was going to be working in the offices instead of the field, she should make an effort to look presentable and ladylike. "Ladylike," She muttered to nobody, "What the hell is lady like about blisters and sore feet".

She ripped off her pink heels and regarded the bottom of them with distrust. "What's wrong with a nice pair of flats? Or tennis shoes? Why does it always have to be heels." She looked down at her leg, and examined her stockings for any tears. A thin white line ran along the back of her calf. She slid an index finger along it, tracing its wondering path down to her ankle. The constant pain and the sight of it were a daily reminder of why she was here, and her friends weren't. She huffed out a sigh and stood up, slipping the heel back on as she did so. "At least I made it back. Not everyone was so lucky, I should count my blessings." she whispered as she adjusted the straps on her heels. Finally after standing up she closed her eyes and took some deep breaths. If she concentrated she could still smell burning flesh.

Natalie Smith was a young woman of twenty-three when she first joined the IRS, now she was just past twenty-five. She had graduated from university summa cum laude with a degree in accounting and a minor in cultural studies. Natalie stood tall at five feet three inches and had fiery red and curly hair which bounced as she walked. Her body was like that of an Olympian athlete except for, of course, her right calf . If you asked her what her best feature was she would say it was her eyes, which were emerald green with light flecks of gold. Her complexion was like a statue made of marble and her expression was hard as stone.

She was a young and supremely talented and capable woman. Though unfortunately, being a woman in today's business world often meant that she got relegated to menial tasks or ignored. Which meant she had to endure listening to her male co-workers talk about "The game this weekend". Or, failing that, hearing them fall silent when she walked into the room. This was almost always due to them discussing their latest sexual conquest. This humored her for very specific reasons. First, because she was without a doubt the strongest psychic that had ever graduated from Duke University. She had taken correspondence courses, of course. Anything else would have given her an unfair advantage. Because of her powers, she could read minds and knew that most of them were lying through their teeth.

For instance, Frank Watkins (A heavy set and balding man) had NOT had sex with a beautiful redhead on Saturday. He had, in point of fact, stayed home and helped his wife of ten years change dirty diapers and watched for the seventy-ninth time a show containing a cartoon pig. And, as a direct result, was considering a total vasectomy within the next few months. Likewise, Michael Jones (a very flamboyant dresser who loved flowers) claimed to have had sexual relations with a pair of blond twins last Tuesday. The truth, however, was two-fold. First Michael had stayed at home with his partner Steve that night and enjoyed a nice marathon of Humphery Bogart films and watering his flowers. Secondly, He was gayer than Elton John in a room full of greased up Swedish speedo models.

The second reason she was so smug was that she knew she was actually the most valued member of the team. Her official title was inter-department liaison. Unofficially she was the head of human relations for the supernatural branch of her work place. As such she was privy to many secrets. Like the fact that the moon landing was real and that the USA currently traded goods with the moon people. Or, that the lizard people did not take over the British royal family. But, instead ruled over the small nation of Kazakhstan near Russia (they also coincidentally made the very best Greek food). And finally that the "director" of the organization that she worked for was in fact no more human than a toaster pastry.

After finally ditching her heels and going barefoot on the tile floors, she arrived at her boss' door. She broke out into a cold sweat as she stared at the stark white lettering on the frosted glass. It read ," Director" and it filled her with dread.. She shook her head and chastised herself for being silly. Natalie squared her shoulders and flicked a perpetually out of place lock of curly red hair over her shoulder. She slowly knocked and waited for the reply. "ENTER FLESHY MORTAL BEING NAMED NATALIE", a voice seemed to seep sickly out from the door. As soon as she heard the voice she could feel it blanket her mind. It felt like the voice burrowed into the pores of her skin and left her mentally naked to its touch. She coughed softly and entered the dark room. Within the room was a horribly large undulating mass. It towered up to the ceiling and was writhing like it was alive, it was the Director.

It. Was. Disgusting. Its mass reached up to the vaulted ceiling of the room. Long moist and mold colored tentacles seemed to jut from its form at random and it had to have had thirty eyes and twice as many mouths. Each of them were a difference size and shape. Its body produced a mucus with an odor like year old jock straps that were soaked in the anal excretions of a skunk. Its tentacles flailed wildly but not violently, as if they were hands moving about constantly. It was tall stinky and morbidly obese, it was the Director.

"FLESHY CREATURE HAVE YOU BROUGHT ME MY SUSTENANCE?", the Director boomed in a thick, almost comedically so, British accent. "Two sugars no cream?" she said as she extended the cup to the large monstrosity. "YES... DID YOU LEAVE THEM A TIP?" the creature said as one long tentacle snaked down and gently took the coffee from her hand. "Yes sir, $3.50 exactly." She said with the air of a person who has been through this before. "GOOD, BE SURE TO LOG IT SO WE KNOW IF THEY FAIL TO CLAIM IT ON THEIR TAXES. THEY MUST PAY THEIR FAIR SHARE AND SUPPORT THIS GREAT NATION." "Already done sir, I also brought you a Bearclaw and I have the files you requested" Saying this she approached the desk and laid down the files and a still warm pastry. "MOST EXCELLENT, YOU ARE MY FAVORITE FLESH CREATURE, SPREAD THE FILES OUT AND I WILL MAKE MY CHOICE."

"You are too kind sir, what or who exactly are we

looking for?", she asked while she quickly spread out the files. "A NEW AUDITOR AND COLLECTOR! A MOST PRESTIGIOUS POSITION AND ONE WHICH REQUIRES A CERTAIN METHODICAL WAY OF THINKING." The creature boomed as it drank its coffee. A fat tentacle landed on one file and began to open it and flip through the file, "HE WILL DO EXCELLENTLY" the creature crowed as its voice boomed through the room. "Sir, are you sure? He seems rather normal, nothing different about him." She asked.

"YES! LOOK AT HIS DEAD EYES AND HIS PALE SKIN, HIS BODY LANGUAGE SCREAMS THAT HE WILL STICK TO THE RULES UNTIL HE DIES. HIS SHIRT IS PERFECTLY PRESSED AND HIS TIES ARE DULL AND LIFELESS. HE EVEN HAS A MOUSTACHE, A BORING ONE!... YESSSSS HE WILL DO NICELY." The creature jiggled sickeningly with gleeful joy. "I will go and collect him then sir," Natalie said as she stood up from her chair, "who should I say we are?" "TELL HIM THE TRUTH. HE SHOULD KNOW FROM THE BEGINNING WHO WE ARE," the Director boomed. "Tell him the truth? Are you sure?" Natalie asked. "YES," The creature boomed. "TELL TOBIAS W. SCHMIT

THAT THE INTERNAL REAVENUE SERVICE HAS NEED OF HIS SERVICES." An hour later Natalie left the building and headed for the most boring place in the world. She was riding in her taxi on the way to the airport and staring at the file when she muttered to herself in a voice dripping with a mixture of both dread and irritation, "Who the hell lives in the middle of Kansas?".

(WINTER)
CHAPTER ONE

Case # 0
IN WHICH TOBIAS TRIES TO HIT A GNOME WITH A SHOE.

IRS

CASE FILE
PROPERTY OF THE UNITED STATES OF AMERICA
DESIGNATED : Security clearance level Omega

"People are, in general, boring.", Natalie thought idly as her plane landed in Kansas. "And the most boring people on the earth live in the most boring place on the earth, Kansas. And in Kansas, there is a place which is the most boring city, WhiteVille. And in WhiteVille, there is a street which is the most boring street in the world, John Smith Street. And on John Smith Street there is a house numbered 123. This is the most boring house in the world.", she muttered under her breath to nobody in particular (or so it seemed). After getting her luggage into the trunk of the rental car and then loading another slightly smaller suitcase. She climbed in and turned the car on and listened to the steady hum for a minute. She looked at her phone and loaded up the GPS. "OK," she said while entering the address into the car's GPS and pressing enter. "Make it so," she quipped with a small smirk thinking of captain Picard from Star Trek. The GPS began to glitch and squeal like a stuck pig. After a few seconds of its hellish screeching the machine also started to spark violently. Then as quickly as it started it sputtered out and died. She stared at the GPS for a second and laid her head on the steering wheel with a loud exasperated sigh."....Shit". She turned around and looked into what seemed, to most normal people, be an empty back seat and said. "Do you know how to get there?"

The house she was talking about stood at exactly two stories tall. It was made of red brick, and sat flat on the ground. The front door was white and it had two windows on the first floor and two windows on the second. These windows were framed with blue drapes and covered with Venetian blinds. The yard was a muted green color and cut to exactly 1.4534 inches in height. There was no backdoor or backyard. This was because the HOA and the designers felt that it would've had too much potential to be exciting. On the door there was a simple handle made of brass and polished to a gleam. The house itself was, in a word, immaculately boring.

This house was the home of one Tobias W. Schmit. And at this moment in time, Tobias was sitting down on an old wooden chair in his kitchen. He was getting ready to drink his morning coffee[*] and eat his breakfast. Breakfast, which he considered to be the most important meal of the day, consisted of two pieces of bacon (burned black) and a slice of

* made his own special way, a recipie for wihich is found in the index

buttered toast with three eggs sunny side up. He had just stabbed a piece of egg when a loud knock came from his front door. His eyebrows shot up his face at sub-sonic speeds and almost collided with his hairline. Tobias stood up and wrapped his well-worn blue flannel bathrobe around him and shuffled to the front door. Slowly he reached for the handle and felt the cool metal meet his grip.

It is at this point we should make a note about Tobias's appearance. He was not a tall man or a short man. He was absolutely average in every way in regards to his size (in every sense imaginable). He was a Caucasian man with black hair and brown eyes. He wore large glasses with thick black metal frames, and sported a very well grown Charles Bronson-esque mustache. On his days off, he wore a white shirt with a brown and gold tie and a green sweater vest with tan khakis. In the morning he preferred to wear a blue flannel bathrobe with a white t-shirt and gray sweatpants. His favorite coffee was a mild brew made from freshly ground French roast coffee beans, with exactly half a teaspoon of cream (a recipe for which is in the index of the book).

Tobias was also average when it came to his intelligence and physical fitness. His preferred hobbies were solid color stamp collecting and collecting paint samples. As well as feeding his goldfish. It is considered a minor miracle that the goldfish was still alive at the time of these stories, and continues to be so to this day. Many scholars believe the goldfish has only remained alive for two reasons. First, because Tobias took excellent care of the fish. Secondly, because the fish was so accustomed to the boredom of Whiteville that the concept of death was simply too exciting for it.

When it came to working it should surprise nobody that his job was incredibly boring. The job was to measure the size of corn kernels for popcorn bags. This consisted of filling out a form for each kernel in the factory. The factory in question created just under 234 thousand popcorn bags a day. Each bag had 50 kernels exactly, as per regulations put in place by a regulatory oversite commission on popcorn. Averaging out to 11,700,000 pieces of paperwork per day. This, in turn, averaged out to 4,270,500,000 pieces of paperwork per year. Tobias loved this job with a passion that most women only long for.

Tobias's hands finally closed around the door handle and opened it at an average speed. "CONGRATULATIONS! YOU HAVE WON A FABULOUS PRIZE!", boomed the man standing on his front porch, who was holding a large oversized check. Behind him stood television crews and a few of his neighbors. Tobias glanced at the check and then at the man, who was standing there grinning stupidly. He wore a plaid suit and his slicked back hair which gleamed in the morning sunlight. His obviously fake teeth were like a large white billboard. "No thank you," said Tobias curtly, "I don't want a prize but thank you for thinking about me. Now please leave before I call the police as you are loitering on private property." Then Tobias slammed the door in his face and returned to his breakfast.

Tobias was slowly raising a piece of bacon to his lips when a second knock came from the door. Tobias stood up and un-hurriedly brushed his clothes off as he muttered angrily to himself. After a moments consideration he walked to the front door and opened it. "Would you like to hear about our Lord and Savior Jesus Christ!?" said a small peppy woman who was wearing a conservative starched white blouse and a small gold necklace with a cross on it. In her hand, she held a well-worn copy of the bible to her chest. Tobias stood there for a minute considering his options and then said, "No, get off my property." And forcefully slammed the door in her shocked and offended face.

A short while later, Tobias was washing his plate, and loading his dishwasher when he heard a loud authoritative knock . He started towards the door and stopped. "No, I am not going to answer the door. I have already dealt with people twice today and I have no intention of dealing with even more. What happened to Saturday being the day of rest? Besides I am not going to fall for any scheme or psycho religious bullshit, what do they think I am? wet behind my ears?!" He thought as he twitched in irritation. It was at that precise moment his eyes fell upon the valve for his sprinkler system. He smiled as his hands circled the valve and slowly turned it counterclockwise.

While he was doing this the knocking continued steadily, even as the water began to hit the front of the house. Tobias raised an eyebrow at this. "Usually this works pretty well... whoever it is should have left by now or at least started cursing." He muttered to himself as he increased the water flow. Then as his curiosity grew he let go of the valve and began to approach the door.

He watched in both a kind of horror and fascination as his hand circled the doorknob and pulled it open. Outside stood a woman drenched to the bone and staring daggers at him. "Tobias Schmit?", She asked in a way which made it sound as if she already knew the answer. "Yes?", he responded while trying to avert his eyes from how the water had made her blouse cling to her form. "My name is Natalie, I work for the IRS. You do know what the IRS is, correct?" She said, as if speaking to a child. "Y-yes." Tobias stuttered as he backed away from the door gesturing for her to come inside. Meanwhile, in his head, Tobias was thinking two thoughts. First, that he absolutely positively should have not turned on the sprinklers. The second is best explained by one line of internal dialogue. "Holy monkey balls, there is an agent of the friggin IRS in my figgin house!!" Natalie stood in his hallway and stared without blinking at Tobias with a sense of unwavering irritation and dislike, her eyes flashing with anger at her current state.

Natalie was the first to break the loaded silence. "Do you have a washroom Mister Schmit? I feel it would be more appropriate to have this conversation later. As in, when I am no longer dripping water onto your floor." She said with a sharp huff of exhalation at the end of her sentences. "Of course, it's right down this hall and through the first door on the left...towels are under the sink." he said with a spasmatic wave of his hand. "Good, Wait for me in your living room, I will be along shortly." She snapped as she turned sharply on her heels of her obviously new tennis shoes and began walking back to the washroom, doing so with an almost sensual and dangerous grace about her. Tobias admired her figure until she disappeared from his view. Then he leaned against the wall and took several deep and heavy breaths laced with panic and mania.

It is here that we should examine the most important thing in Tobias's life, order. Tobias loved order and he loved for things to be in order because it lessened his stress. He was the kind of man who would have a panic attack if he missed his favorite TV show or was more than a second late (or early). About this peculiarity, his high school psychiatrist had this to say. "Tobias is a bright boy with very few of the angst-ridden issues which seem to plague teenagers. But, he does suffer from a disorder which causes him to have periods where he becomes unstable. Episodes such as these result from high stress situations. During which he may take drastic and even manic actions to achieve his objectives. Even going so far as to commit extremely violent acts. This can be noted by the recorded incident attached to his case files. Which show that upon discovering Santa Clause was not real he proceeded to grab a giant plastic candy cane and beat a 'mall santa' to such an extent that he was placed into the ICU. It should be noted that if something is stressful in the extreme, he will absolutely become violent." This assessment was turned in by the school psychiatrist to the school board. Who then promptly lost it through a mixture of sheer incompetence and stupidity, as is often the case with school boards and the useless piles of cartilage who staff them. This omission would eventually lead to many people and organizations, to inaccurately assume he was a very boring person. Which, though he lived a boring life, was in fact highly incorrect. He had just simply learned to manage his stress well and had learned to let things slide off him, to an extent.

He headed to the living room and shakily sat down. "OK Tobias calm down," he said to himself. "The IRS is here and you doused them with water. You also probably got noticed checking her out. And you are now alone in a house with an IRS agent who probably wants nothing more than to audit you into oblivion." He chuckled nervously to himself. "W- what could go wrong?....." He laid his head in his hands with an audible sigh and moaned, "I am so screwed, so very very screwed." He started to contemplate getting up and running out the back door when he heard a voice say, "No, you aren't. Though I will be sending you the bill for my dry cleaning." Natalie said as she settled herself into the grey wingback chair across from him.

"T-the-then why are you here?" Tobias managed to say as he regained his composure. "You have piqued our interest Tobias Schmit." As the words rolled off her tongue her eyes narrowed in a feline like manner. "I represent the director of the IRS and you have been chosen to serve your country through service with the IRS." Natalie finished with as a big crocodilian like smile formed on her face. Tobias wished he had a door to slam in her face, a reinforced twelve inch thick stainless steel bank vault door. "What exactly do you mean?" He asked , squinting with both suspicion and caution.

"Specifically? That a new position has opened in a special branch of the IRS. And, you're required to report with me to the IRS and fill the position. I have already informed your boss of your impending job change. Consider it like being drafted into the armed forces." Natalie finished with a self-secure smile. She liked jobs where the work was done quickly, simply and with absolutely no room for error. "And I guess I have no choice? No chance to say..... be a conscientious objector?" Tobias asked with a sardonic little grin. Natalie let out a small puff of air, "No, of course you have a choice."

Natalie said as if speaking to a mentally handicapped person. "But, if you refuse our offer then we will be forced to call in all your government-sponsored student loans."

A chill ran up Tobias's spine like a finger made of ice. "My loans? As in my over two hundred thousand dollars loans?" He said glancing down the nearby hallway at the front door. "The very same, though I assure you the job is one you would enjoy. It will include a large amount of paperwork..." Paperwork, that magical word. Tobias had loved paperwork ever since he was a young boy. He loved the order of it and the steady rhythm with which one had to fill it out. He loved the smell of the ink on the pages and the sound of a Microline printer. He loved the feel of the phone's buttons under his hands as he dialed the correct numbers. "What's, the job?", he asked with a wry smile. "Simply put we require someone to handle the more ... sensitive cases that arise with some of our more... special citizens. Basically, there will be a lot of paperwork and a lot of talking but I guarantee you it will be a comfortable and easy job." Natalie said with a encouraging but still predatory smile.

"Well, it is my duty to my country, right? I guess I have to." Said Tobias pretending to be defeated as he internally jumped with joy. "Excellent. Let us drink on it then!" Natalie said as she produced a silver flask and two shot glasses. Tobias balked as she proceeded to pour two shots of a thick viscous and snot colored liquid. "What is that?", Tobias asked with a grimace as the sugary sour smell reached his nose. "It is called Veil Fluid, and your first assignment is to drink this shot.", she said with a smile. Tobias eyed her distrustingly, "so either I drink the shot or I face some kind of terrible financial consequence?" He said to her with a sneer. "Yep!", Natalie said downing her shot in one go. "Well bottoms up," Tobias muttered as he drained his shot. A sickeningly sweet taste flooded his mouth and the room seemed to brighten. He swore he could feel something moving worm like through his veins. Suddenly he doubled over as the room grew brighter and brighter. Pain laced like fire through his stomach and it felt like ants were crawling under his skin. After a minute of hellish pain, he set up and opened his eyes. Natalie smiled at him sweetly, "well at least you survived. I think you will do well." "Sure he will!", said a man's voice from directly beside Tobias on the couch. "But I still don't think he is going to be a good partner for me!" The voice continued.

Tobias slowly turned his head to look down and to his right. What he saw there made his eyes grow wide with fear. A small man sat there at just about half a foot. He looked at Tobias with a sense of disdain. He had a blue tunic with forest green pants and a impressive chestnut brown beard tucked into his belt. "And," the little man added, "I still don't see why I had to wear these clothes. It would have been more professional for me to wear my suit." His eyes were the colors of chestnuts and his face was the ruddy red one gets from heavy drinking. In his small hands, he held a little clipboard and a miniature pen. He turned his head to again regard Tobias causing his cone-shaped hat to wiggle under Tobias's nose.

Tobias looked at the gnome for a second and then at Natalie. "There is a gnome sitting next to me and I think I have snapped ." Tobias said as he calmly took his shoes off. "Nat?", the gnome said in a thick Boston accent as he scooted away. "Hush, Trollum we don't need to spook him. He already drank it so he sticks with us," Natalie hissed through gritted and smiling teeth. Tobias hefted the shoe experimentally and Trollum stood up and jumped to the arm of the couch. "Natalie," Tobias asked with a manic smile, "I ever tell you what I hate the most about gardens?" The gnome stared at him and started to roll up his sleeves. "Gnomes," Tobias said as lunged at Trollum. In mid lung he started to swing the shoe at the gnome in a downward strike. "SWEET LION FIGHTING MOSES!" Trollum screamed as he dodged the shoe.

"Trying to kill a little person with a shoe is really disrespectful!" Trollum cried out in indignation. "You're a gnome! You don't exist, you aren't any more real than Tinkerbell!" Screamed Tobias as he advanced on the gnome. "Tinkerbell?! You saying I look like TINKERBELL!? Oh, it is on you long knee'd bastard! Imma mess your shit up!", the gnome cried as his accent grew thicker. Then with a roar he punched Tobias in the shin. A brief side note here readers about gnomes. Gnomes, though small, have the force and strength of an Olympic grade human weightlifter. And are able to move so fast that the human eye fails to register them. So when he hit Tobias's shin it sent Tobias flying backwards leg first.

Tobias picked himself up off the floor and visibly winced as he put weight on his left leg. Looking around he grabbed a book from the bookcase he had flown into. He brandished his book and charged Trollum screaming (what he would later swear was a battle cry), "EEEEEEKKKKK!!!". It was the same sound one would expect to hear from a teenage girl who saw a mouse. Trollum let out a furious roar and charged him fists flailing.

They got three steps before Natalie pulled two tasers out of her purse. She aimed for a millionth of a second and hit them both square in the chest with a blast from each. They laid on the ground moaning as Natalie stood up and smiled sweetly. "Tobias meet Trollum, you two get to be partners now. And in case you can't put two and two together special citizens means supernatural citizens." She leaned down right next to Tobias's ear and whispered, "Welcome to the IRS sweetheart. You should have taken the loans." At which point he fainted and his world was swallowed in an inky black sleep filled with dreams.

(WINTER)
CHAPTER TWO

CASE #1
IN WHICH TOBIAS HAS TO REPOSES THE THULE
SOCIETIES FAVORITE PAIR OF UNDERPANTS.

IRS

CASE FILE
PROPERTY OF THE UNITED STATES OF AMERICA
DESIGNATED : Security clearance level Omega

Tobias opened his eyes and sat up from his desk. He felt.... wet. He looked down and noticed a puddle of drool left over from his not so brief nap. He glanced around at the paperwork surrounding him and sighed. It stood almost four feet high and three stacks deep. Across the room Trollum sat at his own (slightly smaller) desk. He was surrounded by old scrolls and pieces of ancient yellow parchment, He still had a shoe tread imprinted on his face.

Trollum glanced up from his desk at Tobias and raised an eyebrow. He opened his mouth as if to say something but then thought better of it. It had been this way since they had returned from Kansas to Washington DC. At first, Tobias hadn't been able to control himself around his supernatural co-workers. Now, after some very powerful sedatives and a special debriefing, he was better able to understand the world he had been thrust into.

"The supernatural exists," he told himself every morning as he made his coffee. Believing it with less and less difficulty. "In 1778 the continental congress signed a deal with the royalty of the supernatural world about terms for peaceful coexistence. The supernatural creatures pay taxes and obey certain laws. In return, they are allowed to exist and be considered citizens of the United States." This statement had almost become his daily mantra. And, was something he repeated to himself every chance he could get.

      He looked at Trollum and let out a quiet guilt filled sigh. He felt bad about what had happened when they had first met. He knew he was in the wrong and that and that the right thing to do would be to apologize, but he didn't know where to start. Tobias was deep in thought over what to do when the door to their office slammed open. A man, in the loosest definition, swept into the room. He was tall and painfully thin to the point that it seemed like his clothes were hanging on a skeleton. The skin on his face stretched too tightly around his skull making the veins under the skin bulge out grotesquely. He had one hand skeletally thin hand running through his business style haircut.as he stretched to his full height. The other was wrapped tightly around his coffee mug.

Pointed black nails contrasting painfully with the white ceramic material. His palms were hairy and his eyes seemed bloodshot even as he blinked. He stood at over seven feet tall and he had to crouch slightly even once he was completely in the room. He smiled at Tobias showing off a set of pointed fangs. "Evening wage slaves," the vampire said as he gazed upon them coldly.

    It has been debated among those who know of the supernatural whether vampires would make good managers. The thought process goes like so. Vampires are cold bloodsucking bastards with a fanatical dedication to whatever organization or court they are a part of. They are disgusting and vile, truly the worst undead creatures in the world. They are also sarcastic and snide and look down on the people below them. So, it is often concluded that they are the perfect fit for a managerial position.

    "Thomas", Tobias said through a false smile he reserved solely for managers and other soulless abominations. "What brings you down to our humble abode? More paperwork, or do you have something for us to do? Or have you finally decided to kill us?" Thomas smiled a thin smile that didn't quite reach the corner of his eyes. "Oh sweet Tobias. Being snarky to your manager is a quick way to find yourself doing more paperwork." At this thought a Tobias's heart fluttered and tears of happiness welled in his eyes. " But, as it stands you and your compatriot have been officially relieved of paperwork duty (at this a single tear slid down Tobias's cheek). Miss Natalie has a job for both of you that requires an IRS agent." After saying this Thomas turned around and started to leave. Tobias wiped his eyes and glared after him. Thomas paused with one hand on the door way and turned to speak over his shoulder. An action which wasn't unlike a falcon looking back at a rabbit it just flew over. "Oh and Trollum, please keep your fanatic little friend in line."

As the door closed behind him Tobias noticed Trollum had gone a little bit pale. Even his normally ruddy complexion had paled to light pink. "You, ok?", Tobias asked with a hint of concern in his voice. "Yeah...damn it.... yeah I'm fine," Trollum said as he composed himself. "Vampires wig me out. I don't know if it is the way they are too thin to seem alive or the fact that their hands are freakishly thin and pointy." At this Tobias smiled, "Isn't that a bit racist? Or at least speciest?"

Trollum, who was busy adjusting his tie, stopped and stared at him with incredulity. "Yes, I suppose it is. But let me ask you this, why is that a bad thing? Vampires are bloodsucking monsters. The lore says they were originally created by one guy committing a mortal sin. Their very existence is unnatural. And it took the stupidity of a human government to give them citizenship."

He paused and slipped a pocket square into his breast pocket. Then turned to face Tobias. "His kind hunted and killed other sentient races for millions of years. They should have been killed off, but one moronic politician said that they should be allowed to live and now here we are." Tobias balked at this a little bit and looked at Trollum. "I just don't like the fact that they drink blood." He said in a slightly startled tone, the candor with which Trollum spoke shocked him. Trollum turned around and looked him in the eye. "You need to read up on your lore. They don't just drink blood, they also destroy the people they feed on. They invade their minds and break them in such a way that it can't be fixed." Trollum paused and fidgeted with his tie, "And we are just lucky enough to have one for a manager."

Trollum finished fidgeting with his suit and pulled a small hat box from his desk drawer. Tobias noted that it seemed like it was brand new. "Well, then I have two questions. First, why does he work for the government? Second, is that a new hat?" Trollum looked at him and then back down to the hat box. "The answer to your questions are simple. First, Thomas is allowed to work with us because he has an inhibitor implanted in his heart. If he tried to feed on any of us or harm anybody the inhibitor would explode. And small shards of mistletoe would pierce the inner walls of his heart. Thus, paralyzing him and allowing for decapitation or cremation."

Trollum paused and lifted the hat out of its box and examined it. The hat in question was a brown fedora with a blue jays feather in the band "The answer to your second question is, yes this is a new hat. I bought it during the early twenties on my first day with the Internal Revenue Service. I always wanted to be a field agent and be out in the weeds with people like Elliot Ness." Trollum paused as he lifted it up and sat it on his head, it fit him perfectly. "But they sat me behind a desk. All because I have a unique talent for reading other languages. Since then I've gone into the field a grand total of three times. Always to help other agents work out contracts and deals.

"Now I'm going on a mission of my own, so I feel like it's time to finally wear this." He looked at Tobias, daring him to say anything about it. "I think it looks very good on you." Tobias smiled softly as he extended his hand to Trollum, "Tobias W. Schmit, I am your new partner." Trollum looked from the extended hand to Tobias and then he smiled and clasped it in his own. "Trollum Einswald, a pleasure to meet you, Tobias."

Later, after getting lost within the labyrinthine confines of the IRS, Tobias and Trollum found themselves outside Natalie's office . Trollum stepped forward to knock when the door swung open and Natalie gestured for them to enter. The room was sparsely decorated. On her desk were small trophies and a steaming mug of hot coffee. A computer sat against the wall, steadily humming away softly. "Sit down boys, we have a lot to do and not much time to do it." She gestured with her hand at two wooden chairs facing her desk. They all set down and Natalie began speaking. "This is a very very simple mission. You need to repossess an artifact from a secret society while they are at the national Republican convention."

Tobias leaned forward and steepled his fingers, "Are they a threat to the convention? Do we need to fight them?" he asked with a very serious face. Which transformed into a confused look when Natalie started laughing out loud. "No, no... they are running the convention." She said after calming down. "They're called the Thule society. They were a secret Nazi society based in Hapsburg Germany during World War two. The thule society was so well known that even Hitler was a member. They were deeply involved with dark science and the mystic arts. After the death of Hitler they brought their collection of magic infused artifacts here. In return for sanctuary for themselves and their families they agreed to pay taxes on the artifacts to the tune of one billion a year (per artifact). Of course, once they were in America they became politically involved. Then in 2016 they took over the Republican party." She paused only then noticing the slack-jawed expressions of Tobias and Trollum.

"What? You didn't think normal people would elect a reality tv star to be president, did you? I mean did you really think a normal human being could be that conceited and that stupid?" She stopped and composed herself. "Anyways," she said flicking a piece of hair back over an ear. "The Thule are defaulting on their payments in regards to one of their most prized artifacts. Hitler's crotchless panties, and garter belts." She paused here as Tobias and Trollum had erupted into laughter. They laughed so hard that they shook the old wooden chairs they were sitting on.

"Look I know it's funny." Natalie said, trying to

calm them down. " But, these p...articals of clothing are very dangerous. Anyone who wears them gains the charisma and charm of Hitler. Apparently, he claimed that they made him feel like the person he was meant to be. And, they imbue anyone who wears them with the same power." She stopped and waited as Trollum and Tobias calmed down. "Both of you are on the first plane to Nashville, Tennessee. This is where they will be holding their convention and where the Thule will be meeting. They will be disguised as the Southern Baptist Theological Party. Who will, in turn, be a cover for the Ku Klux Klan.

Who in turn will be a cover for the Thule Society of America. Any questions?" Tobias quickly raised his hand to ask a question, "How will we infiltrate them?" This question earned a glare from Natalie, "We are the IRS. We don't infiltrate, you will approach the head preacher. And, with the full authority of a federal agent, say you are with the supernatural auditing department of the IRS. And, that you need to speak with his boss. It should all work out from there." Tobias and Trollum both nodded when she finished speaking and then they all stood up.

Natalie followed them to the front door of the building. "Good luck guys, you are my first agents to send out into the field. Don't disappoint me." And with that, they left for the cancerous sprawl of Nashville Tennessee. The flight was a short one, as things go, and the two agents were happy to touch down at Nashville International. They exited the plane and picked up their bags and checked into the cheapest motel they could find. Then they headed off to the convention.

They arrived at the building in which the convention was being held. It was a large grey convention center. The walls were a dull lifeless concrete gray. Even looking at the building made Tobias feel like his very essence was being sucked away. They made their way to the area where many of the attending political organizations had set up booths. Then they headed down the main thoroughfare. It was here that the loudest and most ignorant members of the Republican party had set up their booths.

They walked quickly past the NRA booth. Tobias noticed that some people around the booth were speaking in Russian. There was one man with a sun burned neck who was screaming, "MUH GUNS PERTECT MEH FRUM DE GUBERMENT MEN! I'LL SHOOT DOWN A GUBERMENT SETTELITE WITH MAH TWELVE GAUGE! YEE HAW AND YEE YEE!" with all the zeal and fanatical volume that is a trademark of religious nutjobs. A man turned to him and said in a thick Russian accent, "Here comrade, vote for your glorious leader. Make Rus...America great again." And handed him a red baseball hat with white lettering.

They passed the table populated with members of the Pro-life movement. They were mostly middle-aged women with "may I speak to your manager" haircuts and blond highlights. Many of whom were talking to anyone and everyone about how they had six or seven children. One woman approached Tobias and started into a spiel while holding her baby, "SIR! You seem like a good Christian man. Sir! Do you want them evil demons to get sweet babies like mine sir? Did you know that forty-nine million abortions happen every hour sir? Don't you want to stop this sir?! Look at my baby sir!" At this, she tried to forcefully shove the baby into Tobias's arms. Tobias, wasn't having any of it and gently pushed the baby back into her arms.

"Madam!," Trollum said as he walked towards her. "I do not give one iota of a crap about you or your baby or any crotch nugget which has fallen from your inbred family tree. I support safe access to abortions and especially birth control. And, after seeing how you act your parents would agree with me!" he paused here to flip his badge open and shoved it in her face. "And, if you ever try to push your baby into a strangers arms again. I WILL AUDIT YOU INTO THE GROUND YOU INBRED MORON!" He finished the last part while screaming towards her face.

Tobias watched all this with an expression somewhere between surprise and mild annoyance. The woman stared blankly for a second. Her inbred hick brain failing to process what was happening. Then she blinked as if she were waking up and turned away to find someone else to push her drivel onto. After this event, many onlookers gave them a wide berth. Except for the people who were there proselytizing. They tried to swarm them even more. But after Tobias had to pull Trollum off of a member of the Baptist Church who had tried to claim the earth was only six thousand years old (Trollum had become enraged as he knew people who were older than that). Most of them stayed away as well.

Eventually, Trollum and Tobias found the man they were looking for. He was a large and rotund fellow. With shifting beady little eyes which were sunk back into his head. Every few seconds he ran a hand through his receding hairline. When he smiled you could tell his teeth were fake because they were too big for his mouth and gleamed bone white. His lips seemed to stretch thinly when he talked. His hands, like the rest of his body, were thick and chubby with fingers like uncooked sausages and covered in a sheen of sweat. They tended engulfed other hands when greeting people as the palms were the size of a small book.

On his chest, he wore a red tie with a tie pin in

the shape of a cross. To the right of that he had a name tag that said, "William Davis, Head of the Southern Baptist Theological Party." He was busy watching a preacher on the big stage in front of everybody talking about the end of times. Tobias was the first to approach him. "Sir," said Tobias as he approached, "I am an agent with the IRS." Davis turned to look at him, his beady little eyes squinting. "And?" He wheezed as though the very action exhausted him. "I am with the supernatural auditing division. This is my partner Trollum." Tobias replied as Trollum approached and looked up at the man, his face a mask of annoyance. "We need to speak with your boss's boss about an artifact you haven't paid taxes on in about three years. And as your organization is under our purview, we will be re-possessing your artifact." Tobias fell silent and for a moment the only sound was Trollum's pen scratching on the paper of his notepad.

William let out a throaty chuckle and jiggled a little, "Ah can tell you are new to this.... Boys, the Thule society and for that matter the Klan and the SBTP belongs to no man or government and does what we want. You ain't got no right to take our property or our technology. And besides our glorious leader is wearing them right now. So if you wanted them you would have to physically rip them from his body. " He gestured up towards the man speaking on the stage.

"And you ain't gonna do that boy cause you don't have the balls. So now why don't you go back home and tell your boss that there was jack all you could do." He finished in a thick southern accent that seemed to ooze snark and arrogance. Tobias looked down at Trollum who was busy scribbling on his notepad. And then he looked up and started looking around. As he did he noticed that the people around him came from all different walks of life.

There were members from the NAACP (who were not there in any official capacity) and the Sons of the Confederacy standing next to each other. There were some Pro-life groups who were sharing beers with the Republicans Doctors Association. There were even members of the Klu Klux Klan. Who ,while wearing their robes, were talking with the Jews for Republicans Association.

Then, like someone flicking a light switch, an idea formed in Tobias's mind. "So, what you are saying is that he is wearing it right now? As in up there on stage in front of God and everybody?", he asked with a Cheshire cat grin. "Yep, so there ain't nothin' you can do about it," Davis said with a sense of arrogant finality. There was the sound of lead snapping and a muttered curse. Then Trollum looked up from his pencil at the two of them.

"Do either of you guys have a pen or a sharpener? My pencil broke." Davis looked at Trollum with disgust and then rolled his eyes, "Ah gots a pen over here." He said as he turned his magnificent bulk around to reach for a pen in his briefcase. The moment he turned his back Tobias was already in motion and was sprinting for the stage. He pushed past Davis, knocking him over in the process which made Davis flounder like a turtle on its back. "Help me!" Cried Davis, and in doing so he drew the crowds attention onto him and away from Tobias.

The helpful crowd flipped him up in time to see that Tobias had made it halfway through the crowd to the stage. "Get off me, you idiots! And get that man!" Davis screamed at his helpers, who promptly dropped him back onto his back. Then rushed after Tobias while ignoring Davis's screams of impotent rage. The crowd seemed to part as Tobias's pursuers followed him. Tobias was about three feet from the edge of the stage when they finally caught up to him.

He had sat his hand on the stage when he felt someone grab his ankle and start pulling him back. With desperation Tobias reached out and grasped at the air where the preacher was screaming, "AND THE GOOD LORD WILL HEAL YOU IF YOU BELIEVE MY BRETHREN!" The preacher looked down and saw Tobias reaching for him and smiled. His voice boomed from the speakers on the stage, "BROTHERS! Do not stop this man from coming to me! Let him set foot on the stage and I shall bless him in our good lord's name!". And with that, the preacher helped Tobias up onto the stage, and Tobias found himself in the spotlight.

From up on that stage Tobias could see thousands of people. And at the back of the crowd, he could see Mr. Davis wiggling on the ground. He swore he could faintly hear him screeching shrilly at the indignant situation he was in. A voice whispered in Tobias's ear, "Now what long knees?" Tobias freaked out and started jumped up and down on the stage and screamed. "Stop jumping you asshole!", came a harsh whisper from his ear.

He looked at his shoulder and saw Trollum gripping onto it. "How are they not seeing you", Tobias hissed through gritted teeth. "You idiot," Trollum said with a roll of his eyes. "Remember that gunk you drank the day you got hired? That stuff allows you to permanently see through the veil. It means you are able to see me but all they would see is a bit of dust or at most a mouse. The more obvious it is that I am here the more they can't see me." Trollum was about to say more. But, then he had to swing himself to the side when the preacher clasped a hand on Tobias's shoulders.

"BROTHERS! SISTERS! ," The preacher cried in a

loud voice as he held Tobias firmly in place. "Behold! This man is stricken with hallucinations and demons! HE MUST BE CLEANSED WIT THE POWER OF GOD ALMIGHTY!" The preacher looked at Tobias and said, "kneel my child and I shall heal the!" Tobias knelled down and snuck a glance at Trollum and then shifted his eyes towards a nearby fire escape. "Trollum, can you make me move quickly? Like, fast enough to get the hell off this stage and behind a steel door?" He hissed. "Sure, but why? Also, I can almost guarantee you will black out due to the speed." Trollum whispered quickly.

They both looked up at the preacher who was waving his hands in a faintly mystical gesture. "Do it when I give the signal.", Tobias hissed through gritted teeth. "What's the sig-", Trollum started to ask. But, before he could get the words out of his mouth Tobias pantsed the preacher.

The entire crowd went silent.

The preacher was not a well-endowed man. His penis hung down from the evil Nazi panties like a sad deflated balloon. It was gray and wrinkly with tufts of white hair growing around it. His balls hung down to his mid-thigh and looked like two large ball bearings in a gym sock. Then there was the matter of the lingerie he was wearing. It was black lace with a paisley pattern done into the lace. The straps ran mid-thigh and ended in a garter which snapped onto his knee-high socks. At the edge of the panties right below the belly button was a large swastika. Which was bright pink with intertwining flowers instead of the usual red.

The crowd was stunned, and a few things happened at once. First Trollum grabbed Tobias and ran like the wind for the fire door. He knew he wanted to get a large and thick piece of metal between them and what was coming. The next thing that happened would have made Rue Goldberg proud. A series of events was about to happen which would result in the massacre of the century.

A woman fainted.

Mrs. Delores Brown had at a young age

developed a deep set case of severe homophobia and a skilled habit of pearl clutching. Because of this she was at the National Republican Convention to head up a new organization called 'Straight Men for a Straight God'. As such this was the last place Mrs. Brown was expecting to encounter any form of homosexuality, especially cross-dressing.

So when all this happened she fell into a dead faint from the shock. As she fell she landed on her table and caused it to upend itself. Launching pencils and pins and small ceramic Jesus figurines into the crowd. One figurine brained a member of the KKK who had his back turned to a member of the Jews for Republicans. This caused the KKK member to whirl around and punch the Jews for Republicans member across the jaw.

This sent that person flying into one of the Pro-life people, who was carrying a pair of scissors. This person fell forward and stabbed one of the doctors they had been speaking to in the chest. This caused the doctor to scream and run to the nearest group for help. Which was the local branch of the NRA. The conversation which followed went like this. "Help me, I have been stabbed." Screamed the doctor. "YOU'VE BEEN SHOT?!", screamed the collective members of the NRA. "No! I have been stabbed! I need first aid!" screamed the doctor who then fainted from blood loss. "HE BEEN SHOT YA'LL! THERE'S A BAD MAN WIT GUNS IN DE BUILDING!" Screamed the NRA who then began shooting their guns in the air. And, pointing them at random strangers and people who were suspicious (by which I mean people who were not pasty and pale).

Then the whole mess reached the tipping point. When one, particularly stupid, member of the NRA looked at one of their donors and said, "YOU KNOW WHO THE ACTIVE SHOOTERS IS BRUH?" To which the donor gestured around them and said, "Я не думаю, что кто-то здесь является стрелком. Я думаю, что у нас был товарищ. (phonetically: YA ne dumayu, chto kto-to zdes' yavlyayetsya strelkom. YA dumayu, chto u nas byl tovarishch)". Which translates to, "I don't think anyone here is a shooter. I think we are being had, comrade". But of course the NRA member didn't know that.

And as such, he thought he was saying everyone was the shooter. The ensuing bloodbath became known as the Nashville massacre. And nobody noticed a few days later when Tobias snuck in with the cleanup crew. And stole away Adolf Hitler's underwear.

The return trip to Washington DC was uneventful and quiet. However, the debriefing was another issue altogether. "On one hand you managed to retrieve the artifact and didn't go over budget." Natalie said as her nails fell in heavy steady rhythm on the desk. "On the other, you helped to cause the largest massacre in over fifty years." She stared at Tobias and then at Trollum. "But, it isn't your fault. From what I understand that place was full of idiots with guns and religious wack jobs. " She leaned back in her chair and regarded them with something close to a smile. Natalie steepled her fingers and frowned deeply. "And you managed to create a bevy of new ghosts, who will pay taxes to this department. So if it were up to me I would chalk this up as a success." She paused," And it is going to be called a success. But, because people died you have to meet with the director." "Who is the director?", Tobias asked with a cocky grin. After his meeting with the director, Tobias went on to spend the next three days recovering in a psych ward.

Later when he returned to work something had changes. He walked back into the office he noticed that something was tacked to the wall. It was a pink carbon copy of their first mission report. And there was a lot of room on the wall for many more. "Tobias", Trollum said from behind him as he walked into the room and looked at the wall. Tobias turned and looked at his friend. " When I started out here my mentor had a wall full of his case files. I figured maybe we should do the same." he finished smiling bashfully, Tobias nodded as a smile crept over his face. He held out a closed fist towards Trollum and grinned, "Fill up the wall?" Trollum grinned and rapped his knuckles against Tobias's closed fist. "All the way."

(WINTER) - (SPRING)
Inter-Chapter Exposition
Trollums history

-Authors note-
This is just an expansion on the in series lore . It introduces some characters and explains some things. These will take place randomly throughout the stories whenever need be.

IRS

CASE FILE
PROPERTY OF THE UNITED STATES OF AMERICA
DESIGNATED : Security clearance level Omega

The pub was dark and the smelled faintly of pipe smoke. The bar and walls were made out of a dark brown wood that had, over the long years, soaked up the dark smell of the beer. The bar itself was made of one long oak trunk. And, had been carved by hand by the first owner in 1779. Ironically, he still owned and operated the pub. There were no mirrors in the pub. Many of the creatures that frequented its safe haven preferred not to look at themselves. Very well cushioned booths were set back in small alcoves along the wall. This caused them to be filled with deep shadows when unoccupied. However, when they were occupied each one was lit with small oil lamps which had left soot stains on the wood walls behind them.

"The Pub" as it was called by the locals of DC was a place that didn't officially exist. It was the type of place that people tended to whisper about late at night when nobody would hear them. A young man might, on rare occasion, hum to himself a catchy 1950s esque jingle as he shaved, "Oh I am going to the pub tonight, yes I am. To drink without fright, I am going to the pub tonight." in a sing-song cadence. But just as suddenly as he started he would stop and start to wonder what the hell he was talking about.

In the old days people would claim this was the work of witchcraft or sorcery. Some nutjobs today might even claim it was the work of a government agency. The actual answer is that it was just the residual effects of the excellent marketing "the pub" used. As with all things supernatural "the pub" used a different style of marketing. That is to say it marketed within peoples dreams. For monsters and creatures of myth who already live partially in the realm of dreams this meant that "The Pub" was a beacon for their kind. And, it was on a dark night at that strange period between winter and spring, when Tobias found himself inside "the pub" having a drink. Specifically, with Trollum, a kappa named Hiroshi and the leprechaun Tom McGinty in one of the booths at "the pub".

"You realize we look like the start of a bad joke," Tobias said with a drunken smile. "True, but in this business you pretty much always sound like you are in a joke." Tom replied wheezing out a chuckle around the cigarette which hung from his mouth. Tom wasn't very tall (though that is the natural state for leprechauns) but he was very handsome. He wore brown dress pants with suspenders and a white shirt with the top three buttons open. He had his black boots perched on a chair sticking out from the edge of the booth. His hat, a small newsboy cap, hung limply from the back of said chair. He twisted and smiled a devilish grin at Hiroshi and his emerald green eyes flashed. This caused the contrast of his curly red hair on his pale skin to become even more pronounced. It also stretched his ears out from under his mane of hair and showed that they were pointed at the very tip. "Wouldn't you agree Hiroshi?"

Hiroshi, like all kappa, looked like a human-sized turtle with a deep dip where the top part of his skull should be. In this dip there sat a small amount of water, not enough to fill a jug but enough to fill a medium size bowl. "Indeed my friend. Though it is honorable work and it should be strived to be done with the utmost..." He shot a pointed but good-natured glance at Tobias, "delicacy." Tobias threw his head back and laughed loudly. "I wouldn't laugh if I were you, Tobias," said Trollum as he glared at his beer. "Our next job won't be easy." Trollum looked up at Tobias, "we will need to have a private talk before we start into it this time." Tobias snorted and finished off his beer.

"Trollum," Tobias said as he reached for the basket of peanuts on the table. Like lightning Hiroshi smacked his hand in a motion that was both a reprisal and a grab for the peanuts himself. "Tobias," said the kappa. "This is a serious issue and you owe your partner a modicum of respect." "Aye ," Tom muttered over his pint as it magically refilled itself. "I am the first in line to usually be an insultin' prick to Trollum. But, this is nary the moment to be so. It is serious work you are doing, and Tis' dangerous work as well. The Elvish Royalty and NAADP aint nothing to shake a stick at." he finished and he started to down his beer.

"Tobias," Trollum said feeling that his partner, and friend, had suffered enough. " it's not just that we will be mediating for two very powerful supernatural groups. My adoptive-sister is leader of the NAADP . So you will be the only one who is completely unbiased at the proceedings." At this Tobias balked, "Adoptive sister?" He asked with a raised eyebrow. Tom looked up from his beer. Then turned slowly and fixed Trollum with a shocked stare. "Trolly, you haven't told him anything...have you?" Trollum looked at Tom and sneered, " No, Tommy I haven't... But, maybe I should." He let out a sigh and sank further into the booth. And muttered about how he would need another beer if he was going to discuss this.

As he was about to get up the barmaid came by. She was a slip of a girl, no more than 90 pounds soaking wet. Her blond hair flowed down her back and ended in a long braid down by her knees. She had blue eyes the color of the sky. Trollum gazed at her pale pink lips which were slightly parted and always seemed on the verge of a smile. She was busy looking at her notepad when she stopped at their booth and reached for the now empty chips basket. Tom glanced up at her and smiled a large elfish grin, "Hey, Rapunzel how have you been?" he barked out with a devilish gleam in his eyes. "Tom,

Trollum, Hiroshi and you must be Tobias. A pleasure to see you all as always and a pleasure to meet you, Tobias." She said with a simple smile and a glance in Trollums direction. Their eyes met for a brief and electrifying second that seemed to brighten the room. Trollum averted his eyes quickly and she bit her lip so hard that Tobias was sure it would bleed. Rapunzel sputtered out an excuse and backed away from the table and ran to the bar. She nearly hit a patron on the way because she kept glancing over her shoulder and smiling.

The whole table was silent as everyone stared at Trollum. He looked at everybody indignantly. Then focused on getting the blush out of his cheeks and face. "So you were going to tell Tobias about your history. And, why you are wanting to be extra careful with this assignment," Hiroshi said with a gentle cough. Trollum nodded in Hiroshi's direction and looked Tobias in the face. "Three things you need to understand Tobias. First, I may be a gnome but I have never really known many other gnomes. Second, blood does not make the family. And finally, that even in the supernatural world the worst monsters are made from the most normal creatures." After saying this he took a long sip of his beer and stared into the middle distance. Tom looked down into his beer as if he was ashamed and Hiroshi nodded towards Trollum as if asking him to continue.

Trollum began, " My story, like any other, begins with my birth. It was 1879 and south Boston was full of new immigrants from Ireland. My mother and father had brought 15 kids with them to America and I was the first to be born here. Unfortunately, my birth came at a great cost and my mother lost her life during the process. My siblings blamed me of course but my father did the best he could to keep us together as a family. But, after about a year of not dealing with the pain caused by the loss of my mother, he turned to the drink . He became violent and lazy and by my fifth birthday, we were living on the street. My father made my sisters sell themselves while he made my brothers learn how to steal and rob."

Trollum sighed and looked Tobias in the eyes," I was never good at it. One day, I was breaking into a dwarfish family's apartment a few blocks from our hideyhole. When I felt a hand land on my shoulder. It was Wilhelm Einsvellt, he was younger back then and was strong as a herd of oxen. I was much skinnier and much much weaker. I tried to run but he held me in place with one hand and grabbed my chin and forced me to look up into his face. I still remember how he looked at me from under these large bushy eyebrows. And how his eyes shined through his thick glasses. He said,' Oh laddie, you look like you could use a blanket and some good food. How about you sup with us tonight?' I couldn't move, nobody had ever looked at me with anything but distaste or neglect before. And, here was this man with this crazy white hair and a ridiculous beard and eyebrows. And, he was looking at me like he would his own son." Teardrop big and fat slid down Trollums cheeks and landed with an audible plop on the table. Tobias leaned over and offered a napkin to Trollum, "and then?" he asked.

"What do you mean and then?" Trollum sniffled, "I was hungry, cold and tired. I broke down crying like a child. And all the old bastard did was he pulled me in for a hug and kept whispering, 'your home now lad, your home.' And after that, I never left. That night I met Harriet Einsvellt. When she saw me all she said was, 'tsk tsk boy don't you know your mother was worried about you!' and I said I had no mother. Then she got in my face and leaned in close enough to where I could smell the peppermint on her breath. She smiled in such a way that it filled the wrinkles left by the thousands of smiles before it. 'I was talking about me ,' she said as she poked me in the chest with an old wooden spoon. 'I am your mother now, and if you make me worry like that again I am going to tan your hide'. And... I broke down crying again."

Tobias smiled and sipped his beer, "They sound like good people." "They are," Trollum muttered , "but there is more. It was about a few months after they adopted me and I was outside with my adopted brothers and sister. Who for the record are more family to me than my blood relatives. When, my father stumbled into the playground drunk and with a knife. He saw me and tried to get me to come back with him. I screamed and my big brother Mylum stepped in front of me and pushed my father away. Well, he wasn't having any of that and he started to approach Mylum. Saying he was going to cut him for being such a stupid and filthy brat. So, I tackled my father and pushed him to the ground and wrestled the knife from him. Then cut him across his face."

Hiroshi nodded sagely at this, "And, as I have told you before Trollum. You did the right thing. He was no father to you and in your actions, you saved a life." Trollum smiled at this and nodded his thanks. "True, but you know I still wish we had called the police or something. As it was I never saw my father again. Five days later one of my siblings found me on my way to school. She told me he had killed himself and that I was no longer welcome in gnomish society. This would have sucked and I wouldn't have been able to handle it if it wasn't for my adopted brothers and sister." At this, Tom sat straight up and grinned, "And don't forget your best friend!"

Trollum laughed hard at this and grinned from ear to ear, "That's the truth." He turned to Tobias and grinned, "I met Tom during my freshman year of secondary school. What you would now call high school. Tom's family had left

Ireland less than a year before he started into my class and it showed something awful. His accent was indecipherable. But, luckily for him, I knew some basic Gaelic and we were able to talk pretty easily. I guess you could say I became his defacto translator. But we didn't become friends until one day after school when my brothers and I were walking home. We had just come around a corner when we saw him getting his ass kicked in an alley by a bunch of troll spawn."

Tom started to get up muttering about going to the bathroom but Hiroshi shot his hand out and forced him back down. Tom opened his mouth to protest but a single glare from Hiroshi shut him up. "My brothers and I rushed up to find poor Tom beat to hell and curled up around something on the ground. It was a cat, a small calico colored cat with a nicked ear. When Tom stood up the cat turned around and nodded at us and Tom and then disappeared. It was only later that we found out that cat was a scion of Old Tom the king of the Cait Sith. We took Tom home and my mother cooed and awed over him. It turned out she knew his mother from church and she made us rush to get her. Together they scolded Tom for fighting until he told them why he fought. And then-" Tom interrupted laughing, "You got scolded and whipped because you didn't help me!"

Trollum let out a hoarse and throaty laugh, "Yes we did, and we deserved it. Though it wasn't a week later they found those trolls dead. With claw marks all up and down their bodies. Ever since then every cat has been Tom's friend and we have been inseparable. In fact, it was the two of us who recruited Hiroshi and his wife to the OSS during WW2. And, later recruited him to the IRS." Trollum nodded to Hiroshi, "You better tell this part."

Hiroshi began to speak," During the war, the emperor sent out a decree. That all mythological creatures must serve the empire. He had two rules. First, preserve cultural integrity and help the war effort. Secondly, do not intermarry or interbreed. This was because many of the creatures in Japan could only breed with humans. This wasn't a problem for many except for the Kappa clans and the Tengu warriors. You see, Tobias, the Kappa are a peaceful people. We do not fight needlessly and we mainly want to be left alone. But, many of us were pressed into service as healers and medicine makers."

"Towards the end of the war I was serving as a medic in Tokyo bay. It was during the winter that I received a summons to the mountain fortress of the Tengu clan known as the Yatomoro. It was considered a great honor to serve a clan as respectable as theirs and I accepted readily. When I entered the castle I had no idea what to expect, but I could never have dreamed of what I found. A beautiful young tengu woman was lying on a pallet dying . Her name was Akiri though now I just call her Aki. She had been in a squadron of assassins who had attempted to kill a high ranking member of the OSS. Her healing took almost a month and in that month we developed a close friendship. I loved to watch her fly, the way she shimmered in the air she looked like a spirit from the gods. And that friendship slowly became deeper and eventually turned into something more. I started to see her in a different light and I couldn't keep my eyes off her. On her last day of healing, we shared a kiss. We thought we had been safe but a servant saw us and reported it to her father who was enraged. He attempted to have me killed but I was able to escape and hide in a nearby village's holy spring." Hiroshi paused and regarded his beer with a glare.

"The tengu lords stripped Akiri of her ability to fly by burning her wings and cast her out into the rain and mud. I found her outside of the springs shrine and brought her in and began the process of healing her. I begged her to forgive me for bringing this misfortune on her and she told me I was a fool. 'Any pain is worth it to be with the one you love', is what she said to me. And, we were together ever since. We joined up with the resistance to the emperor and by the end of the war I had met Trollum and Tom and a few years later I accepted a job here. Now I work as a translator and cultural attache, and Akiri works in a bird sanctuary." Hiroshi smiled as he finished his story and took a long sip of beer.

"These are all beautiful stories," said Tobias grinning. "But what does it have to do with why our next mission is dangerous?" "Tobias," said Trollum," I am (by dwarven and gnome standards)barely out of my twenties. My sister was the only other member of my family who was my age. And, who went to college and she now works as the head lawyer for the NAADP. She is a wonderful woman but she is wicked smart. I mean like genius level smart." Trollum licked his lips and glanced around, "If we aren't careful she is going to kick our asses with just her words. But, we can't insult her either because she is my sister. And, I owe her..."

"Oh? and why do you 'owe' her?" Tobias asked as he scraped the foam off a new pint of beer. "Tobias, she is the one who got me started on the track to become an agent. In the 20's I was essentially a pissed off teenager and if it wasn't for her I don't know what I would have done. She started me on this path and now I have to go up against her..." Trollum said with an audible catch in his throat. "How did she help you get started with the IRS?" Tobias asked.

"That's a story for another night," replied Trollum. Who started to blush again as he saw Rapunzel approaching the table, they all had a good laugh at his expense. And Tobias thought that it was nice to have a family.

(WINTER) - (SPRING)
CHAPTER 3

CASE #7
IN WHICH TOBIAS HAS TO
DEAL WITH THE ELVISH ROYALTY AND THE NAADP*
National Association for the Advancement of Dwarvish Persons

IRS

CASE FILE
PROPERTY OF THE UNITED STATES OF AMERICA
DESIGNATED : Security clearance level Omega

The street was dark.

It was well past midnight and all the self-respecting people of Seattle were asleep or behind their thresholds. At the end of the street under the halo of a wrought iron street lamp stood a tall figure. It stood silently and long golden hair flowed out from under its wide-brimmed fedora. When the figure shifted its weight the tips of pointed ears sometimes peeked out from under the brim of the hat. From within the shadows cast by the hat, a brief inhalation made a cigarette burn a bright electric blue. Smoke that smelled like cherries and elderberries drifted into the night sky and sailed off on the cool spring wind. The embers flared up as the figure drew another breath and danced in its bright yellow cat like eyes. For the briefest of seconds, marble white skin seemed to suck in and radiate back out the blue glow.

From down the street a lone figure hurried towards the one under the street lamp. This figure was a stunningly direct and stark contrast to the other. Short and squat it moved along with both speed and grace that belied an athletic soul. The brown duster over its gray pantsuit and newsboy cap did nothing to hide the attractive and vivacious curves. Short hands with delicate fingers moved to fidget with a lock of loose bright red fire colored hair in a nervous gesture. For a moment knocking up the cap to display a face as pale as the moon and an upturned impish nose. Lips gleamed red as blood in the moonlight and twisted into a smile. Then the cap was jammed back down once again masking the face in shadows.

      The taller of the two figures turned quickly and seemed to great and begin talking to the shorter one. The shorter one stamped one of its feet and pointed with an accusatory finger. Its other hand, it placed it on its lower abdomen. The taller figure dropped to one knee as it grasped at a hand and held something out. The shorter figure started to shake and seemed to go ecstatic. The two embraced and kissed deeply. Their passion and their love burning bright under the street lamp. They parted after a minute and went their separate ways. A shadow in a nearby alleyway detached itself from a wall and a tall and slim feminine figure emerged, jotted something on a notepad, and left.

Two days later, it was nine in the evening in Tobias's apartment. Tom the leprechaun and Trollum were over that night and were in the middle of a heated argument. "I am not making him a green suit Trollum! I will make him any color he wants for this damn thing but not green!" Tom screamed at Trollum while throwing a beer bottle at him in a burst of anger. Trollum deftly dodged the bottle and it shattered against a wall spraying beer everywhere. "Why not?! You used to do excellent work with green! Remember the dress you made for my mom?!" Trollum yelled back defiantly while Tobias rushed to clean the wall before it stained.

"I do, but that doesn't change a damn thing! No green!", Tom said with an air of finality. "Guys, I like black. Black would be perfect for a black tie event.", Tobias interjected in exasperation. "Fine", Trollum muttered, "I just... I want to impress my sister ok?" "I know Trollum, but don't forget that no matter what she is your sister and nothing will change that." Tom said gently as he started taking Tobias's measurements. "Besides," He grunted through a mouth full of push pins, "It isn't like she is going to be angry at you for doing your job. Just be careful around those elvish bastards." Tobias winced as tom tightened the fit a bit too much, making Tom snicker softly, "wimp".

"So explain this to me again?", Tobias asked as he glanced at Trollum, "What is this party all about?" Trollum sighed and got up to get another beer. "The elvish royalty are celebrating five years of profit growth. This profit growth was gained through lobbying for tax breaks. And, by disenfranchising the lower class of the supernatural worlds more mythical beings. By which, I mean people like dwarves, gnomes, leprechauns, and pixies. The elvish royal family's political arm aka the NAAEP. Have been lobbying for better tax laws for their companies for years. And, usually, they have gotten them. This has resulted in an unfair favoring of the Elvish Royalties businesses by the current IRS practices." He stopped for a second as if waiting for questions.

"Ok," said Tobias, "So why are we getting

involved? And, why does it have to be so damn complicated?" Trollum let out a wry chuckle. "Because, these actions have made it impossible for most of the magical community to be able to afford basic necessities. Mainly, because they are shouldering the elves tax burden as well. This has led to the NAADP to encourage their members to not pay taxes. They have been taking money owed to us and, have been using it to buy from Dwarvish and gnomish businesses. Now the IRS is losing tax revenue from both sides. But we don't dare prosecute because if we do it would set things off like a powder keg." He popped the top of his beer and took a long swig before continuing.

"As such, The NAADP and the NAAEP. Who work for the Dwarvish Jarls and the Elvish kings respectively. Have agreed to meet and discuss a way to find peace in this economic dispute. Our job is to make sure this happens. Which was made far more difficult yesterday because two major parties received threats. The head of the NAADP (my sister) received a death threat. And, the prince regent of the elvish kingdoms got one too." He tossed his finished beer bottle into the garbage and turned to admire Tom's handiwork. Then he let out a hacking cough , "To answer your other question. It has to be complicated because Elves and Dwarves are both stubborn ass hats. Just like in politics there are idiots on both sides, and that makes it hell on earth."

"So what exactly are our mission 'parameters' then?" Tobias asked as he made a mental note to take the trash out and dust once they were gone. "First, we get my sister and the prince into protective and negotiative custody. This should give us a decent amount of pull will both sides and protection from retaliation by any party while they negotiate. Then we find out who threatened their lives and report them to the detainment ghouls with the CIA's supernatural branch. The poor dumb guys won't know what hit them. Finally, we ensure that at the end of the night an agreement is signed." Trollum smiled as he admired Tom's finished product and Tobias's new more formal look.

"And here I was hoping for more paperwork," Tobias sighed as he adjusted his tie. "Could have taken the loans boy'o," Tom said with a smirk as he poked Tobias with another pin. "So when do we fly out tomorrow?", Tobias asked through a wince of pain. "Four in the evening. But I want to eat lunch so let's get there at least an hour early." Trollum replied as he drained his beer to the dregs and tossed it underhanded into the trash.

They made it to the airport with three hours to spare.

"I'm hungry," muttered Trollum as they finished checking in at the United airlines desk. "We will get something to eat after we get through security." Trollum replied as they headed for the checkpoint. "Also, why do you get to fly as a child? And why was that check in lady such a bitch to us." Tobias complained as they got into the TSA line and he cracked open a bottle of water. "I get to fly as a child because I lie about my age, duh. Also, it helps that I wear a glamour that makes me look like a kid (albeit a hairy one). And she was a bitch because that's just how they are at United airlines." Trollum gestured towards the water, "You are going to want to throw that away. Also before you ask, the reason we fly them is that even though they suck the soul out of their employees and feed them to their inhumanly grotesque executives. They give free fares to the government.... so we fly them."

"Well, that sucks," Tobias said as he started to finish his bottle. "I just think maybe we sh-", a shrill nasally voice interrupted Tobias. "NEXT!," the person at the TSA podium screeched. She was a wizened old woman who's best days were well behind her. She screeched again, "NEXT!" As Tobias threw away his bottle and approached her stand. She brushed a strand of her greasy dirty blond and brown hair out of her face. "Where is your ticket", she said as she leered from her stool. She smiled a sickeningly nasty smile which made her lips stretch disgustingly. "Oh sorry about that, here it is," Tobias said as he held out his ticket. She snatched it from his hand and he noticed how her skin was loose and spray tanned brown. "Sorry isn't good enough! You should respect my position enough to do everything perfectly before I have to ask!". The smell of her breath was made up of cigarettes and cheap mint gum, it was reminiscent of a dead animal. She handed back the ticket with a glare and a puff of breath. Then she started to say something sarcastic, but Tobias held up his finger and interrupted her.

"Miss," he glanced at her name tag, "Brandy... Do you really think I care about you or your job? You look like a reject for the crypt keeper. Your skin is probably one big melanoma and your hair looks like it hasn't been washed in years. You are an absolutely disgusting person." Brandy sat there stunned as he continued. "But I could look past all that except for your attitude. It pisses me off not because you act like this AND work a menial job. But because you treat everyone like they aren't worthy of respect. So, I want you to think about this. After I leave I am going to walk off and continue my life just like before. You will probably keep working here until you finally keel over from either cheap cigarettes or booze. And when that day comes I guarantee you the world will be better for it." Tobias finished, watching as Brandy the TSA agent sat there stunned into a stupefied silence. He then walked off smugly and waited for Trollum on the other side of the checkpoint.

"Jesus man," Trollum said as they walked along the flight gates looking for a restaurant. "You really tore into her." Tobias smiled and nodded, "Yeah. I knew a lady like that in my first real job. She was the bosses wife and she shit on everybody there. When I quit I told her she was the worst person I had ever met. Since then I haven't taken any shit from anybody, and it has been just really great for my mental health." Trollum raised his eyebrows in surprise, "So that's why even though you are sometimes super boring, no offense, you do some crazy stuff now and then?" He asked with a glance at Tobias. Tobias shrugged, "nah that's another issue entirely" and gestured towards a restaurant.

"How about some Italian?", He asked. "Sounds good!," Trollum replied as they walked towards the restaurant. They were seated immediately and spent the next few hours talking until their flight was called. When they checked in Tobias and Trollum noticed they weren't being seated together even though their tickets said they would be. Trollum turned to the flight attendant and asked why this was. "Our policy is to not sit un-accompanied minors with adult men," the attendant droned soullessly. Tobias shrugged and said it was ok, Trollum did not. "So what you are going to sit me next to a woman? Because that is safer?", he said his volume getting higher with each syllable.

"Uh... yes?" the attendant said after a brief pause. "You're an idiot and so is the board of United," Trollum said with a sneer and then went and sat down in his seat. The rest of the flight was uneventful except for when they refused to serve Trollum alcohol. After the flight, Tobias was waiting for him with their rental car and smiling. "So how was the flight little buddy," Tobias said with a silly grin. "Did the little baby get his dinner?" Trollum glanced up at him with distaste. "Screw. You." he said, accentuating the word with a rude hand gesture.

After checking into the hotel they decided to meet downstairs in the hotel's restaurant. By the time Trollum made it down, Tobias was already sitting in a booth and waiting for him. "Ok," said Trollum as he scooted into the booth across from Tobias. "So about tonight... There are a few things you should know about my sister." Tobias raised an eyebrow and smirked, "does she have two heads? Or a giant beard?" "No no," Trollum chuckled while waving his hands, "nothing like that. She can just be a bit stubborn sometimes and she doesn't always make the best life decisions. Also, the group she leads are sorta pig-headed as well." Tobias leaned back as the waiter came by with water glasses and ordered a scotch on the rocks. "So," Tobias said trailing his finger along the condensation of his glass, "do you know anything about the elves?"

Trollum snorted and gave him derisive look, "I know a bit." He took a sip of his water and sighed. His features sagged and betrayed a deep weariness and Tobias got the feeling he had had this conversation with many people before. "Tobias, you have to understand the situation. Many of these elves have been taking part in the manipulation and control of wealth within the supernatural community. And, they wield a large amount of power in the magical world. This has essentially been a mostly one sided economic war that has been being waged for the better part of the last century. And sometimes it hasn't just been economic. The elvish king has lost three sons to riots and countless men to lynchings. And, the dwarvish jarls have lost five of their heirs in the last few years alone when the elvish security forces... 'accidentally' go to far." Tobias studied his drink for a second then he pursed his lips and nodded for Torllum to continue.

"In fact, the issues don't end there. Dwarves have lost many of their patents to elves. And many gnomes have seen their homes bulldozed for factories and stores. There's a lot of bad blood here and I don't really see a way we are going to pull this off." Tobias finished his water and looked at Trollum squarely. "Hey dude," Trollum looked at Tobias. Tobias held out his fist and pointed it at Trollum, "let's fill up the wall." Trollum held his own fist up and rapped it against Tobias's, "All the way". Tobias smiled, "Damn right Tinkerbell". Trollum glared at him and flipped him the bird. A waiter came around as he did so and noticed Trollum flipping the bird. He coughed politely but firmly and said, "Sir, please control your toddler.

And, instruct him on how to act in polite company." Tobias had to pry Trollums hands off of the waiter's neck.

That night the party of the century took place. Of course, all elvish parties were extravagant. But this one was especially so. Tobias couldn't believe his eyes when the limo dropped them off. It took him a moment to adjust since they had been driving for an hour on a dark private road. The main building was sat on a hill and gleamed. Moonlight played and danced along its marble castle like exterior giving the appearance of a castle from a dream. The lawn sloped down from the front of the castle like manor house and ended at a giant and gilded wrought iron gate. At different spots along the lawn, tables were set up haphazardly but in an obviously planned out pattern. The tables were large and made of oak and seemed to easily be over two hundred years old. Silver candelabras illuminated each table with flickering ethereal light and displayed exquisite food and drink as they cast deep intimate shadows. Will o' Wisps floated along in the air briefly illuminating the party guests in a ghostly otherworldly light as they passed.

The guests were either tall and thin or short and squat. The short ones gathered food and clumped together. Some of the short guests played dice and others laughed loudly and boisterously. They reminded Tobias of people celebrating at an Oktoberfest party. The tall thin ones spoke in a low murmur and some even danced like moonlight shades along the hill slope. Their movements were graceful and quick, made even more impressive by their evening wear. Each one of them were clothed in clothes that looked like they belonged in 18th century Vienna. The shorter ones wore more modern clothes and wouldn't have been out of place on the set of a movie about the twenties. Tobias noticed that the shorter guests seemed to point and laugh when a dancing pair would drift by. A pair broke off from those who were laughing and began to dance. Their movements were swift and decisive lacking in classical grace but full of life and vitality, beautiful in a more primal and ancient way.

"Presenting!," A unseen voice boomed suddenly. Making Tobias and Trollum both almost jump out of their skin.

"Agent Tobias W. Schmit and the gnome Trollum.", the voice paused and then in a tone dripping with disbelief, "Who is also a Federal agent! From the Internal Revenue Service!" A smattering of applause greeted them as they descended onto the lawn slowly. A few elves and dwarves bowed their heads in respect. The two agents had made it halfway to the middle of the lawn before Tobias heard someone yell from directly in front of them, "Trolly!!!". A beautiful woman came running towards them at a break neck speed. It was only when she got closer that Tobias noticed that while she was very beautiful she was also just barely over four feet tall. "Hey sis," Trollum muttered while blushing. He turned and faced Tobias with an embarrassed but proud smile, "Tobias this is my sister Catherine."

"Call me Cat," She said while extending her hand. She had her fire red hair in a bun on the back of her head which was held up by chopsticks. This, as Tobias noted, helped to accentuate her rounder features. It should be noted that it wasn't an unhealthy roundness. Instead, it could be said that it made her look even more beautiful. Her marble skin reflected the white moonlight as she held out her hand and shook it a little, expecting a handshake. She smiled as Tobias snapped out of his thoughts and shook her hand, the smile made her upturned impish nose scrunch up.

"So Cat, we need to take you and the prince regent into custody for the night being.", Tobias said directly and with a smile. Cat seemed stunned for a minute then looked at Trollum, "It's that serious huh? I knew the letter was bad but I thought it was a fake." Trollum looked around as if searching for a hidden enemy, "Unfortunately not. We had the letter tested and it wasn't a fake." As the words left Trollums mouth Cat started to look concerned and then nodded, "I'll go. But we need to find Swi'velt first." Tobias cocked his head to the side, "who?"

Trollum sighed in exasperation, "The prince reagent. He was the one who pushed for the deal in the first place." Trollum turned to Cat, "Where do you think he is?" Cat bit her lip, "I can guess but you aren't going to like it." Trollum raised his eyebrow in question. "He is probably in the nursery taking care of the child hostages", she paused and looked at Tobias who had let out an audibly shocked grunt of horror. "Child hostages from both the jarls and the king have been offered. In the event of any murder or death on the part of either party. The child of the murderer or assassin will be killed." Tobias gawked at her, "That's barbaric!" Cat nodded her head and sighed," I agree but until the NAADP is in char-". Tobias interrupted her before she could get started. "I don't care about the NAADP or the NAAEP. Your organizations are apparently useless and incompetent. Because, otherwise we wouldn't be here."

Cat was stunned for a second and then she set her jaw. "You may believe that but we have done a lot of good forcing the elves to listen to us," She said with all seriousness. "Cat," Trollum said, "you are trying to change the law to disenfranchise the elves. That almost makes you as bad as them." Cat face turned red and she started to get angry. Tobias thought she would explode but she stopped herself and then took a deep breath. "Fine," She smiled at Trollum sadistically, "I have a way to get into the nursery"

"Tobias," Trollum whispered. "hmm?", Tobias grunted in response. "If you tell anybody about this I will kill you in your sleep," Trollum whispered from the confines of a baby carrier. "Awww did somebody not get his nappy? Is somebody a widdle bit tired?" Trollum glared up at Tobias as they walked down the hall towards the nursery. Guards lined the hallway, all standing at attention. Tobias looked down and had to stifle a laugh.

Trollum was using a glamour on everyone but Tobias. To everyone else, he looked like a human infant, no more than two months old. To Tobias, he looked like Trollum, beard and all. Except he wasn't wearing Trollums suit or his hat. Instead, Trollum was wearing a baby blue jumper meant for newborn babies and a wool knit beanie. Tobias looked up as they approached and noticed a pair of guards in front of the doors.

"Another hostage?", the elf to the right of the door asked. "Yep," Tobias replied, "One from the IRS." He glanced down at Trollum. "Cute," said the elf on the left of the door. He reached out and swung the door open and a matronly dwarf and a tall blond elf with golden cat eyes met them. The elf glanced down and cooed softly and picked Trollum up and bounced him in the air a few times. "I think I am going to be sick!", Trollum coughed as he bounced up and down.

The elf held Trollum close to his chest and nodded his thanks towards Tobias. "Thank you for trusting us with your child, I am Swi'velt." Tobias nodded at the prince reagent and said, "Do you mind if I call you prince instead? Elvish is kind of hard on the human tongue." The prince chuckled warmly and nodded his head, "of course. Any instructions about the little one?" Tobias looked at Trollum he was shaking his head slowly. "Yeah actually," Trollum froze with his eyes wide open and glaring at Tobias. "Could you change him for me? I think the guards scared him and made him do a number two." Trollums eyes almost bugged out of his head and his face was red with fury. He looked at the prince in fear and panic.

The prince smiled gently and patted Trollums butt. "Of course I can. I will see to it personally." Trollum started to twist and turn, trying to squirm away. "All right that's it I quit!", he exclaimed but it was to no avail, he couldn't escape. Tobias reached down and pinched one of Trollums cheeks and shook it. "I will see you soon." Trollum started to panic. "Don't do this Tobias. I can hear them getting out a diaper! YOU DIRTY SON OF A B- " and then the door closed. Tobias turned on his heel and left to find a place to set up protective custody. He walked down the hall, ignoring the sounds of indignant screaming behind him as he enjoyed the feeling of sweet payback for his bruised shin.

Tobias jammed his hands deep into his pockets and thought to himself, "Where the hell am I going to find a secure room." He wandered the halls for almost a full hour before finding his first unlocked room. He knocked softly on the door and heard nothing. After opening the door he stuck his head in and found himself in the kitchen. Pots and pans gleamed with reflected light and a fire crackled under a stove. In the corner of the room, a dwarf sat surrounded by food, grease ran down his beard in little rivulets. "Uhhh...", Tobias said as they made eye contact.

The dwarf slowly reached for a nearby roll and picked it up, never breaking eye contact. "I am just going to goooo" Tobias said, as he started to close the door. "No," grunted the dwarf as he started to rub the roll on his body. "I want you to watch me." He began to pull up his shirt, exposing his large and hairy gut. "Nope, no. No thank you, GOODBYE!" Said Tobias as he slammed the door shut. He gave himself a good shake and grabbed a nearby chair. Which he wedged it in the door frame until he couldn't move it any more.

He began searching again and soon came upon another room. He opened it without knocking and found himself face to face with an elf leaning over a platter of cocaine. The thin white lines were perfectly neat and straight, Tobias was actually impressed. Then he saw the elf, they made eye contact and seemed to maintain it for the longest time. Then with a sharp intake of breath the elf sneezed and the white powder covered Tobias from head to toe. Tobias slammed the door shut with a shout and brushed himself off as well as he could. He could feel his body becoming jittery and started to get agitated. He sniffed and then sneezed loudly, "Freaking druggie elf." He muttered darkly as he wiped his nose on his cocaine covered sleeve and began to search again,

Tobias quickly found a third room and threw the door open, it was empty. The room was a bedroom, a large red bed sat in one corner under a canopy. Paintings lined the wall showing elvish kings of old in different regal positions. Tobias walked around the room and nodded to himself as he noted its cleanliness and how empty it was. "One way in and out. Enough space to keep them separate and enough room to keep them safe.", he said to nobody in particular. He didn't know if it was the drugs making him talk to himself or if he was just going mad. He walked out of the room and noted it on a his cellphones gps. Then he turned to go and find Cat.

Finding Cat wasn't an issue as the moment Tobias made it to the lawn he could hear her. "You stepped on my foot!", Tobias heard her cry. He started towards the sound and then he heard a reply. A voice dripping with venom and cold as the north pole drifted to him. "Dwarves shouldn't dance, it's a crime against nature." He raised his eyebrows and started walking faster towards the noise. "Why? I like dancing! And I saw the way your little escort was looking at me, I am sure he liked my dancing too", came Cats reply. An inhuman screech of rage went up and Tobias broke into a dead sprint. He made it just in time to see a woman of chillingly inhuman beauty grab a knife from a nearby table and lunge at Cat.

Tobias made a split second decision and dived between Cat and the knife. He felt as the blade slid between his ribs and he grabbed at the blade with his bare hands. It cut into the flesh on his hands and became slick with his blood but he held it fast. Cat gasped and the elves and dwarves both swarmed around the three of them. "That's enough," Tobias gasped as he held the blade a few centimeters from his organs, his blood dripped on the ground and steamed in the night air. The woman's silver eyes were wide and filled with hate. "A human!? YOU DARE STOP ME?!", she shrieked. Before she could say more a younger woman and even more beautiful woman appeared from the crowd and laid a hand over the older woman's. The crowd gasped as a hum of power resonated through the air as their skins made contact.

Tobias was awestruck, she was gorgeous. Her hair was long and silver and reflected the pale moonlight as if it was a mirror. When she spoke her European-like accent cut the night air like the first frost of winter. Amazingly, the part of her hand that she had laid on his chest when she grabbed the blade was painfully, wonderfully cold even through his clothes. She pushed her mother away and stepped between the older woman and Tobias. She looked at Tobias and then down to his wound, "It won't be anything serious." she said with a grin. Then she turned to her mother. She stood up and seemed to become more regal and majestic as she began to speak. "This man is an agent for the government of the United States mother. Any further harm to him would be equal to an act of war on your part."

The older woman's eyes flashed as if filled with lightning. Then they cleared and she nodded her head sharply.

A young man with ram's horns approached her. In his arms, he held a coat made of white fur and he smiled softly. "Darling wife, daughter, perhaps we should make our leave? I have reached an agreement with the king and I feel it is time to go", He looked at Tobias and grimaced. "I am truly sorry for the wound you have suffered on the part of my wife, agent." He glanced to her then back to Tobias in concern. "Ask for anything which is in our power to give and I will give it to you." A startled sputter came from the older woman and Tobias grimaced as the pain started to hit him, the cocaine and the shock were wearing off. "Anything?" He asked looking at the woman who had saved him. She, after glancing at her father, nodded.

Tobias smiled mischievously and glanced at the woman who had stabbed him, "How about I get to take your daughter out on three dates... if she agrees of course." The moment those words left his mouth he could feel the air change and he saw the girls cheeks turn red. Her mother stared agape with horror and started towards him her face contorting with rage. But her father's arm shot out and stopped her, he was smiling as well. A laugh bubbled up from his chest and he nodded his head at his daughter. She turned to face Tobias. "Very well human, I will allow you to call upon me for a 'date' three times", she smiled softly. Tobias stared in shock and then he winced, the pain was coming back and the buzz from the cocaine was gone He began to stutter and wave his hands around, "I was only joking....Don't you think I should know your name first!?"

She smiled and nodded, "I am Lady Frost, princess of the Fae kingdoms. My father is King Oberon of the Summer faeries. And, my mother, is Queen Mab of the dark faeries." She leaned down placing a hand on the area where the dagger entered his skin. He felt a deep cold spread through him and then his pain go numb. "Call upon my name and I shall contact you immediately," She said softly. Then like the frost on the ground, she and her family disappeared.

Tobias let out a breath and started to fall. He felt more than saw Cat grab his shoulder and support him. "We need a safe place to pull that out," She muttered as they headed for the house. "I have one, follow my lead," Tobias replied groggily. They walked for a bit before Cat turned to him and glanced down at his suit coat in indignation, "is that coke?"

Trollum hated babies. Not so much because they were babies but because they were the same size as him. He looked around the gaily painted nursery with disgust and walked over to the prince. He reached down and for the third time tried to adjust his diaper. He was going to kill Tobias for this, painfully. He tugged on the princes pants leg to try and get his attention. The prince looked down and picked up Trollum and started to coo at him.

"Who is a sweet widdle baby.", the prince said to Trollum as he gently bounced him up and down. Trollum frowned in frustration and looked at the prince glumly. He started to mutter the words to break the glamour. But then he noticed the dwarfish matron put down the baby she was holding and reach into her purse. She pulled out a small black and metallic semi-automatic handgun and turned toward the prince. Trollum screamed and pointed, "yes that's the dwarvish nanny." cooed the prince as he turned around.

He stopped cooing and his face fell into a mask of sadness when he saw the handgun. "Why?", he asked in a voice barely above a whisper as he sat Trollum on the ground. "Because your kind has done too much evil for it to be forgiven in one night. Because I know that blood traitor bitch loves you." Sneered the dwarvish matron. "But you know my kinsmen will slaughter all these children," the Prince said slowly. "you do this and you are killing them." The dwarf sneered, "It is worth it to see your kind finally get what you deserve. Besides, at least they will die now instead of later when your father starves the rest of us." The prince's eyes hardened and he grimaced. "That is what I am trying to stop from happening."

The matron smiled a sick grin, "Too late." She started to squeeze the trigger but then she noticed Trollum who was making his way towards her. She looked at him in shock for a second, and that was all he needed. He broke into a dead sprint. Before she knew what was happening she felt the bones in her hand and wrist snap like twigs. The gun fell to the ground. Between her and the prince stood Trollum, his glamour melted away with a hiss. "A gnome?!", She screamed. She took a step forward towards the gun but then one of the other babies sprinted from the left-hand side and punched her in the jaw. It shimmered and revealed itself to be a small pixie with red wings. He turned and saluted the prince, "Torbitz of the summer Faye, hostage for the dwarf lord Skruk the Un-Ending."

    The matron snarled and dove for the gun again and six more babies piled on top of her. Each one shimmered as their veils melted away to display a myriad of races. There were trolls, pixies, wood elves, and even a halfling. They pinned her down and looked at Trollum and the prince, then at each other. Trollum was the first to speak, "Ok, is anyone here an actual child?" Glamours shimmered all over the room until only one normal baby was left. In total there were twenty-three agents from different families and one baby. Most of them were wearing diapers.

The prince gawked at them in shock and then looked at Trollum. "I changed all their diapers," the prince said shakily. "Yep," said Trollum. "I-I touched so much poop.", the prince said as he looked down at his hands in horror. Trollum nodded slowly as he reached into his diaper and pulled out his badge. "Sir I am an agent for the IRS and I need you to come with me to a secure location. As you can see your life has already been put in danger and it is only a matter of time until it's in danger again." The prince was still in shock and just nodded, his eyes glazed over.

Then he stopped and looked at the baby," What about the little one," he asked. Trollum looked around and then at the prince. "We are leaving him with, what I assume to be, a bunch of professional assassins and bodyguards. He will be fine." The assassins and bodyguards all nodded together. The prince nodded and looked at Trollum who had his phone out and was routing their way to Tobias. "Let's go then," the prince said as he looked at his hands. "I touched troll shit," he muttered as they walked off.

Trollum and the prince entered the room and saw Cat sitting on the bed and Tobias leaning against the wall. He had a dagger in one hand and his side was bandaged. He smiled weakly at Trollum as he came inside. "Nice diaper," he said as Trollum walked towards him. "Shut up," he muttered," Did my sister stab you?" "Nah, bitch fairy queen named Mab did.", Tobias said as he showed Trollum his side. "Jesus," Trollum said, "what did you do?" Tobias smirked, "I saved your sister's life. And I got a date with Mab's daughter." Trollums eyes about rolled out of his head. "Is this true? " The prince asked Cat. "Yeah, he really did save my life," Cat said as she stood up. Trollum looked at Tobias and nodded," Thank you, Tobias, seriously."

Tobias just grinned.

The prince looked around and smiled, "I think this is as good a place as any to discuss the terms of our agreement. Don't you miss Catherine?" Cat looked at him and blushed, "I think so too. Guys, I love you both and everything you have done but we need to discuss this in private." Tobias and Trollum looked at each other and nodded. "We will be right outside," Trollum said. "Just yell if you need us," Tobias added as they walked to the door.

Thirty minutes later Tobias and Trollum were still standing in the hall. Tobias was leaning against a wall when Trollum suddenly perked up. "Did you hear that?" Trollum asked glancing over at Tobias. Tobias sat up and strained his hearing and he noticed he could hear... something, "Footsteps?" He had barely gotten the word out of his mouth when a tall elf rounded the corner. He was flanked by two guards and he had a long pointed beard decorated with intricate beds and runes. On his head, he wore a silver crown, that looked like it had been weaved from silver tree branches, and his face showed a permanent look of distaste. This look only deepened when he approached Tobias and Trollum.

"This is my room agents, and as King I demand access," he said in an imperious tone. "You could be Mary Queen of Scots for all I care," said Tobias with a sneer. "But nobody is going in there until your Prince and miss Catherine have agreed to terms. And, have signed paperwork in both groups names." The king's face turned a bright pink and he took a step forward. "They are done now," he said in a threatening tone. Trollum rolled his eyes as he opened the door and stuck his head in. His body went stiff and he immediately pulled it back out, a look of shock flashing across his face.

"No," he said hurriedly. "They are still, ah, discussing things." Tobias turned and eyed him suspiciously. The king raised an eyebrow and looked at them both. Tobias stood firm and looked at the king directly. "Sir I cannot allow you to enter into the room. As long as those doors are closed then you may not enter." Trollum looked at Tobias and then at the king, "yeah what he said!" The king looked at both of them and smirked, "is that so?" He then extended his hand and flicked it making the doors slam open. This happened just as a loud moan escaped Cat's lips, "Ohhhhh my prince! Right there!"

The King, Tobias and the guards all stared in shock. Trollum desperately tried to block their view. On the bed in front of them laid Catherine and the Prince. They were tangled in each other's arms nude. Thrusting upon one another with animal like vigor. Such was their movements that it shook the bed frame and make the pictures bounce on the walls.

"SON?!", screeched the king. The prince and cat froze and looked at them. The king started to approach them and fire gathered in his hands. The prince pushed Cat behind him and fire gathered in his own palm and glowed electric blue. "How dare you bring a dwarvish whore into this castle! And, even worse how dare you rut with her on my bed!", the king screamed. The prince looked his father in the eye and set his jaw.

"Father," he began, "why do you hate them so much? You have no cause to hate those you have taken so much from. They have done nothing to you except survive in the world you have built for them. You call her a whore but I call her my lover. She is beautiful in every way and so are her people. And, that is why, as your reagent, I have ordered that we will put an end to practices which harm their communities." This stopped his father in his tracks and the fires started to die. "W-wh-what?", he stuttered, seemingly deflated.

The prince stood up. He was still nude but somehow seemed more kingly than his father. "And more so, I have bound myself to her cause through both my promises. And, through matrimony, she is my wife. Say hello to your new daughter-in-law father. Even now she carries your grandchild. She is more fit to wear a crown that any elvish suitor you have tried to thrust upon me. It is a shame you will not get to ever see your grandchild though." The king looked up at his son and his face was a mask of rage.

Hot burning tears filled with rage streamed down his face and he screamed at him. The prince looked at the guards, "his highness is not well. Lock him in the nursery and let the men there attend to him." He then turned his back on his father and held Catherine close, never once looking back as the king was dragged off screaming in rage.

Tobias was the first to speak this time, "So did you actually get any documents signed or what?" The prince smiled as he and Cat finished getting dressed. He reached behind a picture frame and pulled out a brown folder. He handed it over to Tobias and nodded, "This is the agreement and check for the back taxes owed by both sides." He looked at Trollum and smiled, "I apologize for the deceit. But I didn't know how you would react to being related to an elf." Trollum snorted and looked at him, "buddy I am a gnome who has a crush on a fairy tale princess. Is best friends with a human, kappa and a leprechaun. And, I was raised by dwarves. It's all just a drop in the bucket at this point." Trollum smiled at Cat and the prince as he and Tobias turned to go. "Besides we are all the same aren't we?" , he said as the headed towards the door. "See you around Cat, love ya!", Trollum called as they walked out.

They were walking down the lawn listening to the party when Tobias stopped. "Trollum," he asked suddenly. "Yeah?" Trollum said turning around. "I have just one question." Tobias said.

"Hmm?" Trollum hummed with a grin. "Do you prefer cloth or disposable diapers?" Trollum looked at him and then grinned, "I don't know, give it a hundred years and you can tell me. Maybe once you are geriatric you won't be such an asshole."

The two agents laughed as they walked away. Neither of them noticed the white shimmer behind a nearby bush or the bloodshot eyes that were filled with rage. Drops of silvery blood fell onto the ground silently as the agents walked away from the queen of ice and darkness. She fumed with rage and anger. A single word slid from between her lips and then dripped like poison. As she said it ice began to form on the branches of the bush making them wilt and die.

"Tobias"

(SPRING)
CHAPTER 4

CASE #23
IN WHICH TOBIAS
IVESTIGATES APHRODITE'S MULTI LEVEL MARKETING
COMPANY.

IRS

CASE FILE
PROPERTY OF THE UNITED STATES OF AMERICA
DESIGNATED : Security clearance level Omega

"PING!", went Rachel's phone for the fiftieth time. She let out a tired sighed and picked it up from the floor of her dorm room. It was another company-wide text from Mrs. Aphrodite. "Why did I ever decide to do this?" She muttered, rolling her eyes. She unlocked her phone to look at the texts. Each one was a nonsensical line of emojis one might find in texts sent by valley girls. Luckily, Rachel spoke valley girl and could easily translate. She dialed Mrs. A's number on her cell. "Hello," a breathless voice answered after the first ring. "Hey Mrs. A, I'm more than willing to be at the show," Rachel said into the receiver.

"Ohhhhh, goody, "replied the voice on the other end. It was smooth and filled with sensuality. If a man had listened to it he would have fallen down and started writhing in passion. As it were Rachels cheeks became flushed. "Now listen to me," the voice began, "this show is going to be huge and wonderful. If anything goes wrong I can't really pull you out of there and he will..." Rachel knew what the rest of the sentence would be. "It's no problem Mrs. A, I guarantee you it will go off without a hitch." The voice purred and Rachel could almost see Aphrodite in her head leaning forward towards her and sliding her hand down.... Rachel shook her head to clear the images from her mind. and said her goodbyes. She had somebody she needed to call. Her fingers dialed the number and a voice answered the phone. "Yeah?" Rachel smiled, "Hey misses Aphrodite. I want to host the show."

"So Princess Frost?" Trollum asked with a smile. He and Tobias were sitting at their desks typing up reports. "Yup," Tobias replied as he clicked print, "I did it on the spur of the moment. "Trollum snorted at that. "What?," Tobias said indignantly, "I can have a sexual side! I like chicks, I can be interested in women." He protested. Trollum looked at him with raised eyebrows then leaned forward on his desk and regarded Tobias with a appraising gaze for a minute. "Nah", He said as he leaned back, "Buddy you have the sexual and emotional capacity of a thimble...with a hole in the bottom"

Tobias was about to offer a scathing reply when the door creaked open. Thomas stood inside the door frame. He was wearing suspenders today and they made him look like a badly strung guitar. "Hello boys," He said in his dry voice. "Hello Thomas," Tobias replied. "Seems like the director decided that you boys did a good job on the NAADP and NAAEP case. Though I think you could have done without causing a coup'. Anyways, I am supposed to tell you to come to Natalie's office." He frowned darkly as they started to get up, "AFTER!... after you finish this extra paperwork." Thomas snapped his fingers and goblins swarmed into the room. Each malformed creature was carrying stacks of paper. "I am off to play some golf," Thomas said as he turned to leave. He turned back around and walked over to Tobias's desk and picked up his water bottle, "No food or drink at work. I will take this and maybe even enjoy it on the golf course" And left.

Tobias looked after him and then at Trollum and smiled. Trollum raised an eyebrow, "What are you smiling about?" Tobias grinned slyly, "That was my emergency water bottle." Trollum looked at him confused. Tobias's grin grew even bigger, "I may have filled it with holy water. Just in case." A look of understanding slowly dawned on Trollum's face. They both started laughing a deep belly aching laugh. Only stopping when Natalie walked into their office.

"What the hell is so funny?" She demanded as they wiped the tears from their eyes. "You will find out in the morning," Tobias replied. Natalie rolled her eye and held out a dossier. "Well, regardless you are both on your way to New Orleans tonight. They both perked up when she said that. "We have a case?" Trollum said as he reached for his coat and hat. "Yep, you are going to a marketing demonstration. It is being held in a conference room on Rue'de Baga street." Trollum grabbed the folder and started leafing through it.

"What are they demonstrating?" Tobias asked lifting a paper up from the file. "Vacuums that suck out your soul? Magical artifacts that change hair color? Steam cleaning machines that actually work?" "Nope," Natalie replied a grin broke out across her face, "Intimate wear." Tobias and Trollum both froze and looked at her. Tobias's face turned cherry red and he looked away from her. Trollum looked at her and raised his eyebrows. "Seriously?," Trollum said as he plopped down into his chair.

"Yep," Natalie replied as she brushed a lock of hair out of her face. "Dead serious, the owner of the company is the Greek Goddess Aphrodite. She has been on our most wanted list for a while. She started up a bunch of multi-level marketing scheme in the late sixties and she has never paid taxes on them. She did this by not actually being employed by anyone. She claims she receives any money as a gift from her friends." She paused and looked at the two of them.

"Your jobs, this time, are to get photographic evidence of the money being handed over to her at the event. Barring that, getting the money itself." Tobias and Trollum looked at each other and shrugged. "That shouldn't be too hard," said Trollum as he leaned against his desk. Tobias nodded in agreement. "Wellllll," Natalie started. "It is a women-only event. And, they will have wards at the entrances. So you will have to go in physical disguises", Trollum eyed her with distrust. "What do you mean disguises?"

Natalie smiled.

"I can't believe it," Trollum said as he and Tobias stood outside of a shop in a New Orleans strip mall. The spring time sun beat down on them, making it a humid and hot day. "I can't freaking believe it," Trollum said again as he stared at the shop's sign. Tobias was staring too. Then he looked at Trollum and then back at the sign. "You don't think it's really them do you?", Tobias asked as they looked at the sign. The sign's neon lights glowed bright blue in their faces. It read, "Presley and Lennon, Costumes and Disguises"

A man hobbled up beside them and unlocked the door. He was an older gentleman with small round glasses and a large nose. He had a bag with a french baguette sticking out of it in one arm. His hair was long and lanky and smelled like pot. He looked them over, "What can I do for you gentlemen?" He spoke with a Liverpool accent as he ushered them inside.

Behind the counter, another slightly older man stood with his hair slicked back. He was busy eating a fried baloney sandwich and watching a small tv. He looked up and then said in a thick southern accent, "Heyyyyyy Johnny boy. You got the bread and bananas?" He stood up and shuffled across the floor. His blue suede shoes moved with the lack of grace that comes from many years of life. On the wall behind him hung a guitar signed with a very famous name. "Yeah," the younger of the two men said as he handed off the groceries.

"You know you're gonna give yourself a heart attack eating like this. You should eat more fresh fruit, maybe some nuts." The younger man moved to turn off the TV. Tobias and Trollum stood in shock. "Careful Johnny boy," the older man said as he stood up. He was wearing white pants with rhinestones and a wife beater. "You're starting to sound like your old lady." The younger man flipped him the bird and the older man chuckled. "Watch it, you're talking to the king baby."

"So, who are these squares?" The older of the two men asked. The one who had been called Johnny looked up and shrugged. "Natalie's men I think." He looked at them and then back to the older man. The older man chuckled, "Well then...What can we do for you boys?" Tobias was the first to speak, "We need disguises sir." then after a moment he said, "You aren't seriously him are you?" He said while gesturing with his head to the guitar. "Keep it under your hat baby. I've been trying to avoid the feds for the last few decades." He said with a chuckle and a wiggle of his hips. "Too many baby mommas claiming to be mine. Nat the cat helped me out with sticking me here with Johnny." He grinned warmly.

"And yes I am who you think I am," Johnny boy said as he pushed past and offered his hand. "But, call me John, please. And before you ask, no. I am not hiding from the feds. I, had to get the hell away from Yoko and her idiotic suggestions on what 'music' is." John smiled and put his arm around Trollum, "Paul still writes me though and we jam once a year." Trollum seemed like he was about to faint.

"So what are we disguising ya'll as?", The older man said. "A woman and something small that a woman would carry around. We have to sneak into a party that is only women." Trollum said as he regained his composure. John looked at his older friend and nodded. It was as if an idea had passed between the two of them. The older man looked at Tobias and then down at Trollum. "How do you boys feel about sequins?"

Two hours later Tobias and Trollum stumbled out onto the street. The door closed behind them They swore they almost hear someone singing,"...and you ain't no friend of mine".

"Well," Tobias said as he admired his reflection in the window of an empty store. "It could be worse. At least I can pass for a woman." He looked down at his body. John and the other gentlemen had placed him in a skin suit. The "suit" was made of one large piece of latex that covered most of his body. Then they had placed some clothes on him and , at Natalie's suggestion, given him a pair of flats. A little makeup and some fake eyelashes later and he looked like a very ugly and manly woman.

"Yeah an ugly one," Trollum snorted. Tobias looked down at him with a sneer. "You really wanna Try to make that comment while you are wearing that?" He asked Trollum. Trollum looked at his costume glumly, "Yeah I guess you are right." They had gotten into a fight over what his costume would be. Tobias had suggested a baby. Complete with a cloth diaper and pacifier. He said it would be perfect because Trollum had experience pretending to be a baby already. Trollum had told him to take a long walk off a short pier. And, had said he wanted to be a Australian pygmy. John had, at that suggestion, stated that he wasn't comfortable with blackface.

The older gentleman had laughed loudly. And then, made a comment about stealing music from black culture. Neither of them had gotten what they wanted. Because just as they were about to come to blows John had walked out of the back carrying a small brown bag and a mask. He had looked at the older gentleman and said," I think this would be perfect." The older man looked at the tag and grinned. Then in a sing song voice said, "You aint nuthin but a hound dog."

Trollum looked down at his costume and coughed. The fur rippled as if there were real muscles underneath it. But, the mask was a bit stuffy and Trollum was having trouble breathing. "I hate this," he said to nobody in particular. "I know... and I'm sorry for what I said back there." Tobias apologized. "and, for what it is worth you make a very convincing chihuahua." Trollum looked upon him from behind his mask. "Thanks, dude, you make a very convincing chick," he then paused. "You're still ugly as hell though." He said half-jokingly. "And you look like a flea-bitten mutt," Tobias said right back.

After walking two blocks they came to the address for the show. Women were lined up outside and waiting to get in. Tobias and Trollum got in line and waited. While they were waiting a man and his Great Dane walked by. Trollum wasn't really paying any attention to what was going on. He was so focused on just being able to breathe inside the large mask that he didn't notice anything was amiss. But, that all changed when he heard a man's voice yell, "Maximus! No!" And he felt himself get pinned to the ground.

Tobias panicked and grabbed at the huge dog. And, started to pull at his collar with all his strength. The dog began to hump against Trollums costume furiously and with vigor. A muffled "Awww hell no!" Came from under it, and a loud snapping sound came from under the dog. It let out a yelp and ran back to its master yelping in pain. Tobias picked up Trollum and whispered in a hushed scream, "are you ok?" Trollum hissed back his voice seething with fury, "I just had to neuter a dog with my bare hands. No, I am not ok. Put me in your purse I will ride in there."

Tobias had just settled Trollum into his purse when the owner of the Great Dane ran up. "I am so sorry," he said with a smile. His body language and general look made him seem slimy and disgusting. "It's ok. " Tobias said and turned away from the guy. "Can I buy you some coffee to make up for it? Maybe take " The guy said as he placed a hand on Tobias's shoulders. Tobias grabbed the man's fingers and whirled around forcing him onto the ground. He twisted till he felt one of them crunch.

"First things first, who the hell do you think you are laying your hand on a woman? Did I say you could touch me? Did I give any signs that I liked you or thought of you as anything besides the idiot who owns a dog that's too big for him?" The man cried out in pain as Tobias twisted a little bit more making his fingers crunch again. The man whimpered and tears formed in his eyes.

"Also, why the hell would I want to go out with you? You didn't help stop your dog and you named him Maximus for Christ's sakes!" Tobias brought his knee up sharply and rammed it into the man's groin. Then he reared back and punched the man across his jaw, knocking him out. It was only then that he noticed the other women in line were all staring at him. Then they started applauding him and a few even yelled , "You go girl!" Rachel had noticed as well and had started walking towards the commotion. But then her radio squawked and she got the all clear over the radio.

The show was about to start.

They entered into a dimly lit room with a stage in the center. At the back of the stage there was a black curtain which blocked the backstage area from view. Rachel stepped up to the microphone in the center of the stage and looked out over the crowd. Tobias and Trollum were quick to notice how confident she was as she walked up to address the crowd. "Hello, ladies!", Rachel screamed. "Who is ready for the toy show of the century?!" The crowd exploded with cheers and screams. "Alright girls but first let me hear those sales numbers!" Rachel yelled with a fanatical enthusiasm into the microphone. Women started shouting out numbers as high as two hundred. Rachel smiled as they yelled and then she motioned for quiet. "All right those are good numbers! Now let's recite the saleswoman oath." She started into an oath about sisterhood. And, about how they were swearing loyalty to this company.

Tobias looked at Trollum and whispered. "I thought we were taking down a Multi-Level Marketing organization? This is a cult, not an MLM." Trollum responded with a hushed whisper," What is the difference? They use the same techniques and skills. The only difference is cults don't try to sell crap products. Or number in the thousands." Tobias looked down at him eyebrows raised, "Thousands? You mean there are more of these things?" The chihuahua head bobbed up and down. "Yeah", Trollum whispered, "Some sell oils and others sell crap makeup or knives. But they are all bullshit. Most are filled with sycophants and morons. Though the worst are the crazy people who believe oils can heal people."

"So there aren't magic cures for diseases? Like, say peppermint oils?" Tobias asked Trollum. "Oh, sure there are," Trollum replied. "But do you really think that the people who discover them are going to have soccer moms from the suburbs sell them?" Tobias snorted at this and turned his attention back towards the person on stage. He thought about what Trollum had said. He turned to ask another question when a woman started yelling out numbers.

Rachel had started giving out door prizes. "Number 493," she yelled as she reached the biggest door prize of all. "Number 493," she yelled in a slightly more panicked tone. Tobias looked at his ticket and realized that he was number 493. "Here ", he yelled as he held up his hand. Rachel smiled, relieved that disaster had been averted, she pointed towards Tobias. "Congratulations, You just won the best prize of all! A full collection of every dildo and vibrator we have on our product line." Tobias stood stunned. The women around him oohed and ahhed. A few women made comments about testing them out. Some broke into giggling fits and couldn't stop. He could hear Trollum dying of laughter inside his handbag.

Rachel was about to beckon Tobias up onto the stage when she felt a feminine hand on the small of her back. "I'll take it from here darling," Aphrodite said as she stepped into the spotlight. The crowd went wild. Tobias had to admit she was beautiful. She had golden blond hair that fell past her shoulders and she seemed to shimmer with every movement. It was as if her face was made up of every beautiful woman's face ever. Here a little bit of Marylin Monroe and there some Audry Hepburn. And then briefly she seemed to look an awful lot like Princess Frost.

"Let's get this party started!" Aphrodite crooned into the microphone as if it were a long lost lover. She leaned back and pointed behind her and the cloth backdrop of the stage opened. There were three podiums. Each held a different piece of clothing. Aphrodite walked up to the first one and held it up for everyone to see.

It was lime green and about half a foot long. She ran her finger along the soft and silky fabric. It was bright green and had a gold 'S's emblazoned on each breast. Then she held it up and pressed a button on a pair of foam trumpet like ears. "Ohhhh yeah baby!," Screamed a familiar fake Scottish accent. Aphrodite began to speak. "With the OgerGasm 2000, your clients will be begging for someone to get into their swamp. It doesn't come with a fiery redhead or donkey sidekick. Though it does come with fake oger ears and over 100 sound clips!" Aphrodite danced over to the next podium as a loud bass beat played.

The next one she picked up was at least three feet long. It didn't bend when she picked it up either. She ran her hand along the steel plated cloth displaying the sleek black carbon fiber expanse. Then she snapped her fingers and two assistants brought a cinder block and placed it on the ground in front of her. She nodded her thanks and placed the garment on the cinder block. She pressed a button at its base, and it began to vibrate and bounce like a jackhammer. It broke through the cinderblock in just under twelve seconds. Aphrodite smiled at the stunned crowd.

"The Jackhammer 4800! Ladies, this one is for the advanced user. If you really don't want to rock your boys world I recommend you back off right now. This bad boy is powered with a recycled jackhammers motor and can go for hours on end." She smiled as a smattering of applause ran through the crowd, while most of the women stared in shocked horror. "Also, if you use for over half a minute. We are not liable for any medical damages." She sauntered her way to the last podium.

Tobias and Trollum looked at each other and slipped around the edge of the crowd. Tobias slipped back behind the curtain as Aphrodite yelled, "And here is the CoochiePulveriser 9000. Five feet of absolute fabric filled destruction." The curtain muffled the applause and the murmurs. Tobias and Trollum stripped out of their costumes. Trollum gestured to a shadowed alcove where they could hide. They looked in the alcove and saw that it stored the pully systems and spare rope. They climbed into the alcove and waited. Trollum muttered, "I am so glad guys don't have these parties." Tobias nodded in agreement and then they were silent.

The show continued for over an hour. Finally, Aphrodite stepped back from the stage and screamed out, "Keep up the good sells ladies! And remember, Sisterhood is only as strong as your sales!" She kept waving until the curtains closed. Then she lowered her arm and the air shimmered around her. Suddenly, instead of Aphrodite's curvaceous form there stood a naked man with curly golden hair. He was barely over five feet tall and had a roman nose. His body was thin like a runner. When he stretched Tobias could see his veins pop.

He snapped his fingers and an assistant with a staff and a briefcase approached him. "Lord Hermes," the young lady said as she passed him his staff. "It's lord Mercury now darling," Mercury said. "Those pedophilic Greeks never appreciated my special place in the pantheon. At least the Romans had a modicum of decency." The assistant nodded as he twirled the staff in his hands. The assistant opened the briefcase to display a large amount of money. "You made over four million this time my lord," she said as he picked up a wad of bills and sniffed them deeply. "Excellent," He muttered to himself.

"However," the assistant continued. "Nobody has placed any orders for anything form todays show except for the first item." Mercury shot her a glare and then rolled his eyes. "What do women know about sexual pleasure." He said to nobody in particular. "Obviously men are the only ones who know what feels good. And bigger is always better, everyone knows that... speaking of stupid women has Mab gotten her cut yet? Or do I need to deliver it personally?" Trollum chuckled at this and whispered, "you think he is projecting some issues here?"

the assistant nodded , "Already delivered sir" The she closed the case and backed away. "You know," Mercury turned to face the alcove where Tobias and Trollum were hiding. "My staff is supposed to have two snakes on it." Tobias felt something wet and slimy slither up his arm and circle his throat. A hiss escaped from the snake's mouth as it settled near his ear. "Tobias," Trollum said as he gestured at his own snake. "I know", said Tobias, "just follow my lead". Tobias walked out of the alcove with Trollum in tow. He stood face to face with Mercury with one hand behind his back and smiled.

Mercury stared and him for a second and then raised a single eyebrow. "You aren't scared of what I could do to you?" He asked with a hint of surprise in his tone. "Oh," Tobias said, "Absolutely terrified. I am scared out of my wits. But I have to ask why you went through all this trouble for this money. I mean you are a god, you could have snapped it into existence." Mercury snorted and jerked his head towards the curtain.

"The money is a bonus. Do you know why these people buy this stuff?" He asked. Tobias shook his head so mercury continued. "They buy it because they are desperate for money and for control. These people would do anything to have any small bit of control in their lives. And people like me, the owners of other multi-level marketing businesses, take advantage of that. Not because we want to make money, ohhhhh no-no. That is all secondary to the main reason."

Mercury spread his arms wide and smiled, baring all of his nude body in the process, "We do it because we want to see these people suffer. These people are nothing to me. But to them I am a god, regardless of how cruel, sadistic or disgustingly evil and deviant I might be. It's all about being worshipped, even by worms like these." He beamed at Tobias, "what do you think of them apples boy?" Tobias stopped smiling and tugged on the rope he had been holding.

The rod holding the curtain up fell to the ground with a crash. Rachel turned around from the conversation she had been having. All the women in the audience did. A naked man stood in front of them on stage. His ass cheeks were directly at eye level and two men dressed in suits were looking at him with snakes on their necks. One of the men was very short and he pulled a badge out and screamed. "IRS you are wanted for defrauding your employees. And for selling asbestos laced sexual wellness products." Some of the women began to scream in panic.

The snakes reared up to bite them but the Tobias bit the snake around its neck first. His teeth sunk into the fatty skin right behind its head. Blood, cool and wet flowed down his chin and he jerked his head from side to side. He kept pressing down until he bit clean through the snake's spine and muscle. Its head hit the stage with an audible and sickly plop. Trollum's approach was simpler and far more elegant, he caught the snake's mouth on the edge of his badge. Then he threw the badge on the ground and stomped on the snakes head repeatedly until blood oozed out from under his shoe. Mercury looked at the two federal agents in shock and rage. Tobias pulled his phone out and said, "say cheese asshole." The phone flashed brightly, illuminating the scene. Mercury threw the briefcase to the side and started to sprint towards the door. He leapt off the stage and rolled into a crouching position and broke into a run.

He made it halfway to the door before Rachel stepped in front of him. She stood there grinning and he stopped dead in his tracks. "Out of my way you bitch." Mercury snarled with spittle flying onto her face. Rachel pulled her fist back and punched him square in the face with her silver ring. He fell backwards, golden blood pouring from a split in his lip. He held his hand up and touched the blood and a look of horror crossed his face. Then he looked at Rachel and started to try to scramble away. She stood over him and looked down, "Lord Mercury I presume? "Rachel said with a sadistic tone as she pulled a golden knife from her purse. "Lady Aphrodite sends her regards, " she said softly and then she kicked him until he flipped over and then she slammed the knife to the hilt into his right eye socket.

Tobias ran off the stage and sprinted to where he saw Mercury go down. He had expected to find him laying on the ground crying. Instead, he found his corpse, golden blood pooled in one eye socket. A silver dagger gleamed in the light. Trollum walked up behind him and clicked his tongue. "Don't let this get to you Tobias." He said , placing a hand on the calf of his friend. "The Greek gods are always killing each other. It is like a constant season of Game of Thrones." Tobias nodded and then looked at the body again.

He turned and ran to the nearest trashcan and violently vomited. He wiped his mouth with the back of his hand. And then he turned and looked at Trollum. Tobias regained his composure and looked around him. The women stood around him, some had their heads in their hands. He looked at Trollum and started to ask a question. "They are crying because this was their last chance." Trollum said, "Some of them spent their last few dollars getting into this business."

Tobias looked around and noticed some of the

women had gone pale and a few still had the tags on their dresses. He turned towards Trollum and said," We can't leave them like this. We need to give them something to get them back on their feet. This isn't right." Trollum hoisted a small black briefcase and smiled. "This should cover it I think." He said. Tobias nodded and started for the door as Trollum laid the briefcase on the floor. "This wasn't as fun as our last two cases," Trollum said as he opened the case. "yeah, well they can't all be winners," Tobias replied. "Besides I have an Idea I think you're going to like."

A few days later they were in a car with Hiroshi. He was driving them along 82nd street to the hospital for the supernatural. "It is good of you to bring flowers to him. I know you hate him but you did cause his current situation." Hiroshi said as they drove along. Tobias held a vase that had a bouquet of flowers in it. Trollum nodded , "you should be ashamed Tobias." Trollum said, "Thomas is a living creature and deserves your respect. You shouldn't have tricked him like that." Hiroshi smiled as he said this and pulled up to the curb for the hospital and dropped them off. "I will wait here for you, don't be too long."

They took the stairs and were soon at Thomas's room on the third floor. Thomas was laying on the bed in a full body cast. He had tried to drink the holy water from Tobias's bottle while he was out golfing. This had, in turn, caused his bones to start to liquify and for him to erupt into flames. It was only through diving into a nearby sewer pond that he saved himself. Thomas's eyes followed them around the room as Tobias sat the vase full of flowers at the end of his bed. His eyes narrowed and he tried to make a comment through the bandages over his face. Trollum smiled and laid a pink slip of paper up against the vase. It was a notice of termination of employment, for stealing an employee's property.

Thomas's eyes bugged out and he looked from Tobias to Trollum. Tobias leaned in and whispered, "Hope you enjoy the flowers, blood boy." And then he and Trollum stood up and left. The air around the flowers shimmered. In their place stood a vase, filled with stuffed animals and lingerie of different shapes and sizes. One started to vibrate and another started saying ,"get out of mah' swamp!". He shook with fury causing the vase to fall over onto him and spill the water onto his crotch. A crotch which was padded with highly flammable bandaging and which absorbed the water quickly. Which was a problem because and the water was blessed by a friend of Tobias's who was a papal priest. Thomas's crotch erupted into flames and he screamed in agony as smoke filled the room, and the world was better for it.

(SPRING-SUMMER)

Inter-Chapter Exposition

When Trollum, Hiroshi and Tobias Triple Date.

IRS

CASE FILE
PROPERTY OF THE UNITED STATES OF AMERICA
DESIGNATED : Security clearance level Omega

All in all, Japanese style roast duck is not a good thing to serve a Tengu. For starters, it's a little bit racist, due in part to Tengus being from Japan. Also since Tengus are avian in nature it is cannibalistic. Finally, it is simply in poor taste. Of course none of this occurred to Tobias on the day He, Trollum and Hiroshi were all scheduled to go on a triple date.

It was a few days after Tobias and Trollums visit to Thomas in the hospital and Hiroshi was still cross with them. "I don't know how to make it up to him," Trollum said as he and Tobias were filling out small stacks of paperwork. Since Thomas had been fired the paperwork had slowed down considerably. Their new boss was a grandmotherly Babayaga, a Russian witch spirit. She was a bit old fashioned, as she had hexed her computer on the first day. And a bit ill-tempered, showed by how she had turned Bill the security guard into a newt on her second day. And tended to drink, she had bought all the vodka in the tri-state area on her third day.

But, she did care for the boys and gave them decently if un-asked for advice regularly. She had advised that

Tobias hang garlic around his home to drive away gnats and salesmen. And she had told Trollum to drink radish juice and carrots if he wanted extra vigor in the bedroom. On more than one occasion she had tried to have 'the talk' with them. She was also more than happy to enable Tobias's paperwork addiction. Doing so by shuffling off all her paperwork onto him. This pleased Tobias and he was happier than a fat kid in a candy store. If he could only get Hiroshi to come around then he would be perfectly content. "I mean it isn't like we involved him in it," Trollum reasoned aloud. "Trollum," Tobias rolled his eyes, "We had him drive the friggin getaway car."

Trollum sighed and inclined his head in acceptance. "Well, what would you suggest," Trollum said as the door to their office swung open. The babayaga was there and she was carrying a pile of folders in one hand. In the other hand, she held a frosted bottle of vodka, it was half empty. "What is bothering," the babayaga said in a thick Slavic accent. Tobias explained to her what had happened, then she started laughing. "Your friend is too uptight! It was all in good fun and he deserved it." she said, dismissively waving a gnarled and wrinkly hand through the air.

"Just take him out for good time. He will come around." The babayaga said, her single dark blue eye flashing from under her heavily wrinkled brow. "He won't listen to us. He will barely even talk to us." Trollum said glumly as he fidgeted with his pen. "Bah!," she exclaimed spitting on the ground as she said it. "You have lady friends yes? Make a big date! Then you ask for forgiveness." Trollum seemed to brighten at that idea and glanced at Tobias. "I can call Frost. A good first date would be a group date..."Tobias muttered hesitantly. After considering it for a second Trollum shrugged . "I could ask out Rapunzel. It would be a good excuse and I know she likes you and Hiroshi." Trollum nodded to himself as he said this. Tobias looked at him and smiled, "A date it is then." Tobias grinned and waggled a raised eyebrow. "Dude don't be weird", Trollum rumbled as he turned back to his work.

Getting a date with Frost was easy for Tobias, he said her name. "Frost, he said as he thought of her. His phone began to play a familiar jingle and Tobias tapped the screen to accept the call. "Hello Tobias," Frost said through the speaker. Her smooth and silken voice sent shivers down his back. He parted his lips to say something but she interrupted him. "You are wondering if I would go on a triple date with you weren't you?" She said with a coy tone. Tobias stopped cold and stared at his phone. Was she spying on him? Did she know what he thought about doing to her at night? Did she have eyes on him right now?

"My grandmother told me you might be calling," she said in a more relaxed tone. "Y-your grandmother?" Tobias asked. "Yes," she purred, "she can see things that most people can't. Past, present, and future, you get the idea." Tobias chuckled, "she must make a killing at the races." Frost tittered with laughter, "Money is not something she considers worthy of her attention." Tobias rolled his eyes. "Don't roll your eyes when I am talking," Frost said sharply.

Tobias looked around wildly and Frost tittered again. "By the by my darling Tobias. The answer is a very solid yes. I would love to go on a triple date with you and your friends." Tobias started to speak but was cut off again, "Your little gnome friend is about to call you. Text me the address of the restaurant and I will meet you there." Frost said, then there was a click and she was gone.

Tobias glared at the phone for less than ten seconds before it started to ring.

Hiroshi had readily agreed to go on a triple date with them. Though Trollum suspected that was Aki's (as Akiri preferred to be called) influence. He, Tobias, and Hiroshi had discussed where to go for a moment but they settled on an Asian fusion restaurant. The name of the place was the "Chair for Men Now!". They had a strange billing system. Where everyone paid an equal share of the group ticket, also they had a red color pallet for their theming. They all agreed to meet there at a quarter to eight, Tobias was there at seven. But, even though he got there early Frost was waiting.

"Tobias," Frost said as she inclined her head

slowly. "Princess Frost," Tobias replied as he took her hand and kissed the back of it. Frost blushed and pulled her hand from his. "How very gentlemanly of you," she said as the blush faded away. "I watched a video. About how to greet royalty," Tobias muttered as he glanced aside. Frost let out a peal of laughter like a bell. "Tobias," she said wrapping her arm around his bicep. "I don't want to be treated like royalty. I want to be treated like a friend and a normal woman." She leaned in and whispered into his ear.

Her hot breath made his skin crawl. His eyes fluttered closed as she spoke softly. "And, I may even possibly want you to treat me as a lover. Later that is." At that last part, his eyes flashed open. Just in time to see Trollum walk into the lobby of the restaurant. Next, to him, Rapunzel stood comfortably. She had her hair braided, as usual. But she also had flowers in her hair. She was wearing a beautiful blue gown and she was blushing. Trollum was blushing as well.

Trollum adjusted his collar as he approached Tobias. Tobias noticed a bright red lip-shaped mark on his neck. Trollum clasped Tobias's hand in his and shook it heartily and grinned. A gentle cough from Frost reminded Tobias of his job. "Rapunzel," he said, "this is Frost." Rapunzel curtsied to Frost and then smiled at Tobias. "So you set your old manager on fire?" She asked with a hint of a giggle in her voice. "Yeah, but he was undead so I figure he probably needed to warm up." Tobias quipped as Frost snickered at Rapunzels comment. Then Hiroshi and Aki entered the restaurant.

They were a study in contrasts. Hiroshi was short, barely five and a half feet tall. Aki was tall standing at well over six and a half feet. Tobias noticed that where Hiroshi had distinctly jutting body angles, as most turtles would. Aki was more soft curves and smooth lines. As she walked her avian feathers shimmered in the light. She moved with the grace of a predatory eagle. And Tobias knew why the Japanese empire had used the Tengu as assassins. Hiroshi smiled as they approached and soon they all stood in a clustered group.

"Before we start I feel like Trollum and I owe you an apology," Tobias said to Hiroshi. Hiroshi nodded his head and smiled, "It is ok Tobias. I know you didn't mean any harm by your actions. And, if we are being honest, after hearing Aki's opinion on the issue I feel you did nothing wrong." Aki stepped forward and looked at Tobias and Trollum, "I do not approve of you deceiving my husband. But, I also feel that your mission was a righteous one. Hiroshi is very peaceful and he does not understand why people like us do things which cause others pain. HE would rather have a peaceful world than a just world. But, I explained to him why what you did was the right thing to do." She smiled and twitched her head towards Hiroshi in a very avian way.

"Hiroshi," she said softly, "don't you have something you want to say to your friends?" Hiroshi coughed softly and looked ashamed. "I am sorry for ignoring you and for being rude." Tobias and Trollum locked Hiroshi in a hug. The expression on his face was not one of comfort but one of severe dislike for hugs. Trollum and Tobias both knew this and hugged harder. They might have hugged Hiroshi all night but their group was called to be seated.

The server directed them to a table with a red tablecloth and red chairs. Once they sat down the Server walked around passing out menus. After she finished passing them out she stood up and smiled as she began to speak in broken English. "You are thanked for coming to 'Chair-Me Now'. Special of tonights is. "Roasted Quackers" and "Pig balls in dumplings" they very good." Everyone nodded their head as she spoke (as one does when being told things by any service professional).

  The server took their drink orders and left them to look over the menu. The women discussed what looked good while the men mostly ignored each other. Then the turning moment of the night happened, the women had to go to the bathroom. As all men and women know there is a fundamental difference. In regards to how women go to the bathroom and how men go to the bathroom. Men are solitary creatures, like a lone wolf in the night. When one announces he has to use the restroom the rest silently agree to not go near the bathroom unless he has returned. Men have died from the fact that they will refuse to use the bathroom together regardless of if they need to or not.

Women are the opposite, they avoid using the bathroom alone. Instead forming into groups like birds called a gossip. Gossips are formed from four or five women. All whom enter the bathroom together and what they do in there nobody knows. Men's theories about this have ranged from crazy to the mundane, The truth is nobody knows. As for myself dear reader, I believe they go to the bathroom together so they can commit a black sabbath to the dark lord of heavy metal and makeup.

The women stood up and Frost began to speak to Tobias. "Darling," she purred in a way that earned a snicker from Trollum. "Order whatever is lightest on the menu for me. I would hate to spoil my taste for dessert... and after dinner distractions." Tobias blushed deeply and nodded. Rapunzel looked at Trollum and smiled, "Trolly you order for me too. I think it would be very romantic and manly." Trollum coughed and nodded. "Hiroshi, order for me please." Aki said almost as an afterthought.

Almost immediately after the women left the server appeared. Her smile seemed almost painted onto her face. As if the long hours on her feet had dulled her brain. And with it her sense of propriety, and the only thing she had left was that smile. "ready to order?" She asked as the men all looked at each other bewildered. "What were your specials again?", asked Tobias as Trollum and Hiroshi looked at him hopefully.

The server looked at him and repeated the specials without the faintest flicker of dislike for Tobias. The men all nodded sagely as she spoke and Trollum coughed a little. In the end, Tobias ordered, after ensuring it was ok with Hiroshi, the roast duck for himself and Frost. Trollum ordered some Japanese style ramen for himself and a plum salad for Rapunzel. Hiroshi ordered a salad as well and a plate of raw meat for Aki.

The men thought they had done well. They thought themselves paragon of manliness and virtue. They thought they were the smartest men in the world. They were so very very wrong.

The women returned just as the food was being delivered. Frost slid in next to Tobias and whispered, "Apparently Trollum and Rapunzel have gotten a hotel room for the night. I hope you weren't as presumptuous as to do the same?" Tobias coughed in surprise, nearly choking on his drink. "No of course not!" He protested after dabbing up a few drops of liquid with a napkin. "A pity," Frost said as she eased back into her chair. Tobias glanced at her his mouth half open. "I'll say no more on the topic, Tobias Schmit. Just know you could have had something amazing for dessert if you had chosen to take it." She smirked as she said this.

The dishes had all been placed before everybody and the servers gathered around to remove the lids. They all counted down and then removed them at once. Everyone stared at their plates in astonishment. Rapunzel turned and looked at Trollum, her face red with anger and embarrassment. "Are you trying to say something? Do you think I need or want to eat a salad?" She said, her volume rising higher with each syllable. Trollums face, on the other hand, grew paler with each syllable. Frost coughed politely and looked at Tobias with raised eyebrows, "Roasted duck?"

Tobias looked at the duck and then to her. "I like duck, and I wanted to share it with someone I cared about." He looked at her meaningfully, meeting her gaze like a schoolboy looking into his crushes eyes. Frost breathed in sharply when their eyes met. Her cat-like eyes contracted and her breathing seemed to speed up and she smiled a cool quite smirk. "I am flattered that you would share it with me then", she whispered almost to herself.

Aki smiled at Hiroshi and swallowed a piece of meat. She tore and pecked at it like a bird and Hiroshi slowly chewed his, and Rapunzel's, salad. Rapunzel smiled at him as he ate and then looked at Trollums bowl of noodles and smiled at Trollum. "Well," she said as she picked up her chopsticks. "At least we can share these noodles with each other." As she said this a piece of bloody and raw meat flew through the air and smacked her in the face. "Oh my god," Aki said with a squeal, "I am so sorry. It is a bit hard to eat neatly when you have wings." Rapunzel laughed it off and pulled the piece of meat off the table and turned to ask the server for a paper towel.

The server stared in horror at her for a second and then ran into the kitchen. They all froze and watched as the chef stepped out from the kitchen and approached the table. He turned to address Rapunzel and spoke smoothly and calmly. "Madam, I would like to apologize for this but I suggest you leave." Rapunzel was aghast and asked why they should leave. "The chef coughed and said," You just took a piece of bird meat to the face, a thigh I believe. I think it would be best if you went and sanitized yourself so as to not catch salmonella." At this Aki interrupted him, "Excuse me was that bird meat you just fed me?" she asked in a cool dangerous voice. The chef turned and looked at her with a squint. "Yes, what of it?", and then all hell broke loose.

Aki lept from the table and stalked towards the kitchen, her talons curled into fists. Hiroshi started to follow her as she began to shout curses in Japanese. Trollum and Rapunzel looked at each other and ran for the bathrooms to take cover. Tobias and Frost sat there dumbfounded as a bloodcurdling scream came from the kitchen as Aki stalked through the door. Tobias grimaced and looked at Frost and jerked his head towards a nearby booth. They ran to the booth and took shelter there in each other's arms. Tobias was shocked to find that Frost was warm and soft in his arms. And that when she buried her face in his chest he could smell the lavender in her hair.

The aftermath of the situation was three casualties (the chef and two servers). The shuttering of the restaurant due to the destruction. And, the mutual agreement that from now on they would only eat home cooked dinners. This led to an interesting agreement between the group. That they would all meet at Trollums house for dinner during the last week of August.

The group parted ways and Frost turned to leave. "Frost," Tobias said suddenly. She turned around and looked at him expectantly. "Frost, I like you... a lot. I haven't ever felt like this towards anyone before and I need to know. Do you like me? Can you even like a hu-" Frost cleared the space between them faster than he could blink. In a flash, her lips were on his.

His mind went blank and he lost himself in her. She writhed on his body like water caressing the beach. Her lips tasted like frozen berries and her hands felt like cold silk on his neck. She broke the kiss and stared deeply into his eyes. "Of course I like you. You are the only man to ever stand up to my mother like that. You are willing to die for your friends and you didn't back down. The question is do you like me enough to last two more dates?" Tobias stared at her and she smirked as she untangled her hands from his hair. She stepped back and he took a deep breath. "I wanna make a bet," he said slowly. Frost's eyebrows shot up and she inclined her head for him to continue.

"If I make it three dates you have to spend one night with me." As he said this the color rose in her cheeks. "And... If you enjoy the night you have to go on as many dates as I want with me. Possibly even one every day." Tobias finished looking her dead in the eyes. Frost stood up straight and met his gaze fiercely. "Very well Tobias, you have a bet." And like that she dissolved into snow.

Tobias hacked out a cough and waved his hand through the mini snow flurry. Then he began to walk down the street into the night air. Somewhere in the distance, a lonely street artist played a tune on an even lonelier trumpet.

(SPRING-SUMMER)
CHAPTER 5

CASE #28

IN WHICH TOBIAS

CONFRONTS PIXIE MOONSHINERS.

IRS

CASE FILE
PROPERTY OF THE UNITED STATES OF AMERICA
DESIGNATED : Security clearance level Omega

"Oh my god!" Tobias screamed. "I've gone blind!" Hot tears began to stream down his face and fall to the ground. "No, you haven't," Trollums familiar grumble filled voice sounded close. Tobias reached around blindly and soon found purchase on what felt like a beard. "Tobias," Trollum said slowly, rage barely concealed in his tone. "Yeah?" Tobias replied cautiously. "First Tobias you need to open your eyes," Trollum said slowly but with force. Tobias gripped harder on the beard, gaining a grunt of pain from Trollum. With his free hand, he slowly forced his eyelids apart. His face took on a gray pallor as he saw what he was gripping onto. "Secondly," Trollum growled in a low voice, "Let go of my pubic hair."

Tobias looked at his friend's fury filled face, "What the hell happened?"

"We are going after what?" Tobias's voice was filled with disbelief. "a group of pixies led by a goblin, who are running an illegal whiskey distillery." Trollum replied with a grin, "Just like Elliot Ness!" Tobias looked into his coffee and grunted, "so

.....moonshiner pixies?" Trollum nodded heartily, "not just moonshine, they are also stockpiling drugs and growing pot." Tobias's eyes bugged out of his head as he spit up some coffee. "Shouldn't the DEA be handling this? Or, well, anybody else?" Trollum's smile grew even bigger, "Nope! We are the only branch of the federal government that deals with the supernatural." Tobias sagged in his chair and looked like he might have a panic attack. "But it isn't like we won't be going in without back up," Trollum said as he realized his friend was getting worried. "We already have a man on the ground in the area, his name is Bubba." Tobias looked at Trollum sullenly, "what kind of hick name is Bubba?"

Bubba, as it would turn out, was a very very 'hick' name. That evening Tobias and Trollum flew out from Washington DC and headed for Knoxville Tennessee. They spent the flight discussing the conversation Natalie had had with them that morning. "Boys," Natalie had said, "This is a big job. Bigger than anything you have ever taken on. We have been after the tricky bastards since the very beginning of the IRS. Your jobs are simple, get in and serve them papers. And then get out alive with the carbon copy. Bring it back here and deposit it with us for use in eventual court proceedings." They both quickly came to the conclusion that this was going to be a very interesting mission, and then Trollum rolled over and went to sleep. As Trollum drifted off to sleep Tobias lovingly stroked the paperwork in his lap While doing this Tobias stared out into the inky blackness of the night as they flew and thought of Frost.

By the time they landed the sun was shining and the morning fog was just thinning. Tobias and Trollum stumbled groggily out of their gate and came face to face with the strangest person either of them had ever seen. He was at least seven feet tall and had suntanned skin, well wrinkled with age. He smiled at them displaying that he was missing three teeth, the rest were obviously about to follow. "Howdy ya'll," Bubba said as he extended one large hand. His eyes were bright green and flitted across Trollum and Tobias's face. "Ya'll ready to do some pixie huntin?" Tobias froze up and Trollum shot Bubba a look. "Mister Bubba," He began, "please refrain from referencing the supernatural in public. It is a need to know situation." Bubba smiled another toothless grin and smacked Trollum on the back. "Buddy folks around here don't really give much of a damn. Besides, the supernatural is pretty normal around here on account of these mountains. Now let's go get yall some grub." He half led and half dragged Trollum and Tobias to the luggage pick up and then he escorted them to the parking lot.

"Which one is yours," Tobias said cautiously as he eyed the pickup trucks that populated the parking lot. "Awwe trucks are for pussies," Bubba waved a hand in the air and then spit some tobacco laced spit onto the ground. "I'm parked at the back," he pointed to the other end of the parking lot. Trollum, who had been pulling his luggage behind him, began to curse loudly and emphatically. Bubba smiled and started to walk.

"So ya'll gonna stay for the Smokey Mountain Ball Bash?" Bubba said over his shoulder. Trolum let out a huff and wiped sweat from his brow, "The what?" "Ball Fest?" Bubba stopped and stared at Trollum in shock. "It's a really famous festival we have around here bouts! Ya'll have to stay for it!"

Tobias arched an eye brow and grinned, "What is it?" Bubba shrugged, "We have a bunch of carnival rides and eat bull and bear testicles." Tobias and Trollum stared at Bubba in horror. "YOU EAT WHAT!?" Trollum screamed. Bubba didn't seem to notice the tone of Trollums voice and shrugged, "Balls." Tobias shook his head and smiled, "Nah man I think we are good." At this Bubba shook his head and started to walk, "Yall don't know what you are missing."

They walked for what seemed like hours until they finally reached the back of the parking lot. Big rig eighteen wheeler trucks and RV buses surrounded them. "Which one is yours?," Trollum panted as he leaned against his luggage. "It should be around here somewhere..." Bubba muttered. He walked a few rows in front of them and then looked to the left and exclaimed, "Well shoot! There it is!" And then he slipped between two RVs. Trollum and Tobias rushed to follow him when they squeezed between the large vehicles they were not prepared for the sight that met their eyes. "Well, what do ya think?" Bubba said with another toothless grin.

"It's a....." Tobias started as he stared. "It's a freaking tank!," Trollum screamed as he stared at the monstrosity before him. The tank was an old Sherman tank from WW2. It was painted orange and white. A 'U' & 'T" were interlaced on the front of the tank and blazed brightly in the sunlight. Bubba leaned against the barrel and grinned. "Yup," he said, "She's mah, baby. Bought her used and with four cases of ammo." At that Tobias scurried to the side of the tank, "It can actually fire?!" He squeaked in a cracking voice. "Yup, don't have much more ammo though. Fired most of it off." Trollum climbed up onto the tank and glared at him. "At what or who did you fire?" he asked. "Oh you know, Florida fans mainly I also fire at pixies whenever they get near my property." Tobias looked at Trollum who was staring open-mouthed at Bubba. "Well," Tobias said, "Let's get loaded up."

They tried to get Bubba to drop them off at a nearby hotel but he refused. "I'll drop you boys off after we get done strategizing for tomorrow." He said as they rolled along on the side of the highway. Cars passed by them, some even honked and waved. By the time they reached a restaurant where they could sit and talk privately, the sun had set.

"All right," Bubba said as they sat down to eat. "The situation is about what you would expect. These damn pixies have been causing trouble in the mountains for nigh on a hundred years. Our job is to finally serve them with legal papers. Hopefully, we will be able to do it without any bloodshed, but I ain't too hopeful." Tobias raised an eyebrow, "Why do you say that?" Bubba snorted, "Cause they have a friggin goblin on their side. Damn thing is the size of a bear and about twice as mean. But with Y'all, I think we have a shot. They're holed up in a holler about two miles from the entrance for the park. There is only one way in and one way out from there so it should be a quick and easy job." They would have continued on talking, but then the waitress brought them their food. The rest of the night was divided between eating, discussing what gear they would need. And Trollum trying to figure out how to eat fried chicken with a fork. Instead of his fingers, which he described as a "savage way to eat your food."

The next day Trollum and Tobias met Bubba on the outskirts

of the Great Smokey Mountain National Park. "That's all ya'll are wearing?" said Bubba who was wearing a camouflage outfit with two Ar-15 assault rifles akimbo style. Trollum gestured at his immaculately kept suit and smiled, "What's wrong with it?" "Well for one," Bubba said holding up his fingers as he listed off the reasons. "You are gonna stick out like a sore thumb. And for two, we have a three-mile hike and you are wearing dress shoes. You sure you want to go in that?" Trollum chuckled and rolled his eyes, "I have walked over thirteen blocks in these shoes, I will be fine." Tobias looked from Trollum to Bubba and grimaced. "I think I will take a pair of boots."

An hour later, and once Trollum admitted he was wrong, Bubba gave Trollum a pair of boots and a salve to help with his new blisters. They hiked for what felt like an eternity before they came to a small clearing. The sun shone brightly upon the forest floor and would have made the place perfect for a picnic. If it wasn't for the five shirtless pixies and piles of trash that surrounded them. Each pixie was barely over a foot tall and wore a pair of overalls. Patches covered every inch of their clothes and they were barefoot. Tobias watched as one of them smiled, showing a shiny lonely tooth. The smiling one punched his neighbor in the arm. This quickly descended into a scuffle on the ground, their wings shimmered as they rolled in the dirt. "Dewdrop! Sunshine! Get your white trash asses up out of the dirt and help me stir the mash. Screamed one of the older looking pixies. His wings were like those of a black butterfly and his features were worn and drawn with either age or drug use. The pixies jumped up and screamed, "Yes sir, mister Flutter!" They rushed around the clearing as Flutter ordered them around. He would point and scream an order and then like lightning it would be done. In less than five minutes the mash for the still had been stirred, the pot had been watered and the acetaminophen had been unloaded.

"Alright," Bubba whispered, "wait for my signal and then we move in." "They are shorter than me, "Trollum protested. "Why can't we just move in right now, we can take them." Bubba grimaced. "No, we can't. Trust me Ya'll will be happier and more alive if we do it my way." Trollum was starting to get irritated, "What the hell are you talking about? Besides what do you know, you're nothing but some mountain hick." Bubba's face turned red and he glared at Trollum, "Fine you want to be in there so bad?" He grabbed Trollum by the back of his shirt. "Hey! What the F-" Trollum screamed as Bubba threw him in a perfect football spiral. Trollum flew screaming through

 the air and right into the face of the oldest pixie.

The pixie fell back gripping his nose and screaming. "What in the hell was that!' He yelled as blood streamed down his face. Trollum stood up and brushed himself off. "Sir," Trollum began "I am an agent of the IRS." He pulled a copy of the paperwork and shoved it at the pixie, "You have been served. Please sign her-." Tobias watched as one of the pixies swung a shovel at the back of Trollums head, knocking him out in one blow. "Shit! Bubba what do we do?" He turned to see Bubba was gone. "Well you have a purty mouth don't ya," something growled from the underbrush. Tobias felt the hairs on his neck rise. He had the brief sensation of something flying towards him at an incredible speed then he only saw darkness.

"Tobias," Trollum growled. He was louder this time and obviously more pissed off. "Let go of my pubes." Tobias had to mentally force himself to let go and then they sat there. Trollum was sitting across from him and reclined on their cage walls. "It's about time you woke up," he said. Concern crept into his voice as he continued. "After they knocked me out the goblin must have gotten the drop on you." Tobias shook himself and rubbed his shoulders, "The goblin?" Trollum jerked his head in the direction behind Tobias. Tobias then slowly turned and looked at the group of creatures behind him. The Pixies were busy loading a truck with crates and equipment. Leaning against the truck bed was a creature that looked like a cross between a bear and a crocodile. It's beady eyes watched carefully as the pixies loaded the truck bed with their equipment.

"Got any idea what they plan to do with us?" Tobias whispered to Trollum. "No," Trollum squirmed uncomfortably. "As far as I can tell they plan to either kill us or leave us to rot." As he was saying this a shadow fell over the two agents and they looked up to see the goblin towering over them.

"Actually," the creature said in a gravelly voice. "We are planning on handing you over to our partner. And letting her take care of you." The goblin sneered, "I know the queen would love a chat with you especially Agent Tobias."

The creature spread its arms and stretched. Its ear twitched as somewhere in the distance a car horn played a part of the song 'Dixie'. " But," it began, "Maybe we can have a littl-" A hole appeared in the goblins chest and it let out a gurgling scream. Seconds later hits head exploded in a fine mist. "Holy Shit!" screamed one of the Pixies, just before the truck turned into a fireball and engulfed them. Tobias and Trollum threw themselves flat onto the ground as the goblin's corpse fell through the wall of their cage. Its blood oozed out and turned the ground a sickly shade of black.

"I told ya'll we should do it my way," shouted Bubba. His voice echoing strangely due to the armored tank. "You freaking redneck!," Trollum screamed as he and Tobias stood up. The barrel of the gun swiveled down to face Trollum. "I'm sorry did you say something?" Bubba asked sweetly. Trollums face went pale and he looked like he might throw up. "I said you're freaking amazing!" He yelled as he started to sweat. "That's what I thought," Bubba said as the barrel swiveled around to face forward. Bubba poked his head up out of the tank and smiled at them. His smile quickly turned into a frown as he noticed neither of the two men were wearing any clothes.

A shopping trip later the agents and Bubba were standing outside the airport. "Natalie is not going to be happy," Tobias sighed as they checked in with the airline. "Yeah, well Natalie is rarely happy isn't she?" Bubbas half said and half laughed. Trollum turned to look at Bubba, "You know Natalie?" Bubba bit the inside of his cheek and nodded, "Ahhhh you could say that she's my sister." Tobias almost coughed up a lung from shock. "Yeah, I know it's shocking, ain't it? Well, she was always the brains of the family. I was always more on the physical side of things." Bubba hacked up some spit and swallowed.

"Listen, boys," Bubba said, his voice taking on a pleading tone. "When you get back north could you talk to Natalie for me? Could you tell her that what happened in Nebraska wasn't her fault? And regardless of the past that her family still loves and misses her?" Teardrops welled up in Bubba Smith's eyes. Tobias placed a hand on his shoulder and smiled. "sure we will." Bubba smiled and shook their hands. And then they flew back home.

That evening Tobias knocked on Natalie's office door. "Natalie," he said as he stepped inside. "Yes, Tobias?" Natalie said as she leaned back from her computer, "We need to talk about your family." Natalie's brow furrowed and she grimaced. "Ok but we also need to talk about something else." Tobias looked at her, his face a mask of confusion. "Yes, about 'the queen'. The Pixies partner, we think it's Mab." Tobias stood there for a second and frowned, "Shit."

(SUMMER)
CHAPTER 6

CASE #30
TOBIAS ATTENDS A JOB FAIR... IN HELL.

IRS

CASE FILE
PROPERTY OF THE UNITED STATES OF AMERICA
DESIGNATED : Security clearance level Omega

Hell was, as far as Tobias was concerned, not deserving of its bad reputation. Sure it had a lake of fire, much like the priests had told him when he attended Sunday school as a child. But what they had failed to mention was the fact that Hell also played host to a multitude of five-star restaurants. And that the beach along the lake of fire was a popular vacation place for the dezins of the supernatural world. "And," he reflected in a muted whisper, "it's even nicer when the government was paying for it." Tobias raised his drink to his lips and took a long sip. Letting out a long sigh, enjoying the feel of the ice-cooled drink as it slid down his throat.

"Trollum are you almost ready to go?" he said over his shoulder as he leaned on the balcony of their room. They were on the thirty-fifth floor and from there he could see the whole of the lake of fire. He watched smiling as a small family of demons lounged on the beach. A little child played with a fire drake in the firey surf. "Hey Tobias, did you pack any sunscreen? Mine expired in the seventies." Tobias turned to address Trollum and had to stifle a laugh.

Trollum was wearing a Hawaiian print shirt with wooden buttons and white cargo shorts. In his shirt pocket hung a pair of aviators and a red pen. He was also wearing bright white knee-high socks and open-toed sandals. But, the coup de gras of his humorous ensemble was his hat. His whole head was almost hidden under his wide-brimmed straw hat. On anyone else, the hat would have simply looked dopey. But on Trollum it gave him the appearance of a mushroom made out of straw.

Trollum raised an eyebrow as Tobias started into a coughing fit meant to disguise his laughter. "Oh like your outfit is so much better?" Tobias straightened himself up and looked at Trollum accusingly. "What's wrong with my outfit?" He gestured at himself. "Tobias," Trollum started, "You are wearing Kahkis and a sweater vest, in hell." Tobias just stared at Trollum, not comprehending or not regarding the slight jab his friend just made at him. Trollum rolled his eyes and asked for the sunscreen again. After applying sunscreen to every inch of his skin Trollum was finally ready to go.

"I haven't ever been to a mixer, are they any fun?" Tobias

asked Trollum as they waited for the hotel elevator. " This is hell Tobias, it's always fun." Trollum stopped to carefully choose his next words. "But, it almost always has a way of biting you in the ass. That's the problem with hell. IT is a lot of fun but it also makes everything worse." Tobias thought on this for a second as they loaded onto the elevator. "Then why are we at this job fair then?" Trollum sighed and toyed with his name badge. The badge was bright blue and had a cartoon devil on it. It read, "Convention sponsor and recruiter. IRS"

"We are looking for creatures to fill the evilest jobs in the world." Tobias smiled, "And what kind of jobs are those?" Trollum turned to look at him and smiled in return. "Tax Accountants and lawyers."

They were on the sidewalk outside the hotel waiting for a cab when Tobias asked his next question. "And I'm guessing the best ones come from Hell and that's why we are here?" Trollum coughed out a laugh, "No the most soulless and disgusting lawyers and accountants come from, in descending order. Yale then Harvard and the Princeton. But we can't afford to pay their salaries. So instead we come to the next best place, Hell. Besides, the accommodations here are better for us. Fewer creeps." At this point, the Taxi pulled up and they climbed into the back seat.

The taxi cab peeled out from the curbside and accelerated into traffic quickly. Trollum jabbered on about Hell and how it had become a place for recreation and college education. Tobias, however, was instead focusing on the cab drivers name. "Excuse me," Tobias said as he rapped on the cabbies divider. "Ja?" The cabbie said looking into the mirror. "I am sure you get this all the time but are you Hit-" The cabbie cut Tobias off with a wave of his hand. "Ja Ja, I don't do autographs." Tobias looked at Trollum whose eyes had grown wide as dinner plates. Tobias leaned forward again and smiled ruefully," So garter belts or stockings?" The cabbie seemed to stiffen up at this and then relaxed after a minute. "Garter belts, Disney is the one who wears stockings." Trollum broke into a coughing fit and Tobias's eyes bugged out of his head.

They would have gone on but the cabby pulled into the

parking lot for the Dark Prince Convention Center and Spa. "that will be fifteen dollars," The cabbie said. Trollum leaned forward. "Mind if we pay you in deutchmarks?" The cabbies brow furrowed and his little toothbrush looking mustache began to twitch with barely controlled rage. "Get the Scheiße out of my cab" Tobias and Trollum quickly stepped out of the cab and onto the sidewalk. Behind them, the cab peeled out and they swore they could hear someone cursing in German.

Trollum rolled his neck until it popped and they approached the convention center. It was a distinctly modern building. Interlaced with a cobweb of steel and carbon fiber. The windows were tinted so black as to be reflective. And somewhere in the distance, an industrial strength air conditioning system hummed. Tobias and Trollum entered into the building through a row of large black glass doors. Once inside the building Tobias was struck by how cold and immaculately clean the lobby was. "I could live here," he said to Trollum as he ran a finger along a wall. "Don't get used to it," Trollum growled. He jerked his head towards a table marked registration.

As they approached the table Tobias began to curse his choice of careers. Behind it sat a demon, but this one was nothing like the others he had seen. She wore a pants suit that clung to her ass like paint. And her blouse was so tight that he thought it might burst. The top three buttons were loose and happily showed off her ample cleavage. Her skin was red like fire but seemed like it would be soft to the touch of his hands. "Or to the touch of other things," he caught himself thinking lewdly. She smiled a dazzling smile at him and asked for his name. But he couldn't take his eyes off of her curvaceous figure long enough to answer.

Trollum coughed loudly and punched Tobias in the back of the knee. The pain snapped him back into reality and he smiled and said they were with the IRS. The demon nodded and bent at the waist to get their nametags. Tobias felt something start to stir within him and it took all his will power to force himself to look away. Trollum took the ID tags from the young demon and thanked her. And then he half dragged and half walked Tobias to a nearby water fountain. "Get a drink" He growled.

The moment his lips hit the cool flow of water from the fountain Tobias suddenly became aware of his immense thirst. He also became aware that he was on an adrenaline high and that he had broken out in a cold sweat. "What," he panted, "What was that?" "That," Trollum replied, "was a succubus. A young one and one meant for humans." He eyed Tobias carefully and then frowned in thought." What?" Tobias said as he took another sip of water. "They aren't supposed to use them for receptionists at inter-species meetings, it almost goes against our agreements. Someone might be trying to get to you." It was Tobias's turn to raise an eyebrow.

"Who the hell, no pun intended, would be doing that", he asked incredulously. "Well, succubuses tend to be part faerie. That's how they slip through into the human world so easily and are able to reproduce with humans. SO, I will let you guess who it might be." Trollum waved his hands through the air in an exasperated expression. Tobias frowned and gritted his teeth, "goddamned Mab. What is her problem with me?" Trollum let out a sharp breath of air and shook his head, "Pick one, you are dating her daughter. You destroyed her deal with the elves and you ruined an MLM scheme she was helping to run. Oh! And you killed off the majority of her old sorority." Trollum counted each reason, raising a finger for each one. Tobias shot Trollum a look and then smirked and turned his face upwards, "I was acquitted of that last one." Trollum let out a bark of laughter, "So was OJ buddy. So was OJ." Tobias frowned and nodded.

"In all seriousness," he said, "is there anything I can do about it?" Trollum leaned against the wall and bit the tip of his pen. "No," he said after a moment's thought. "Not really, Mab isn't known for negotiating with mortals. You know her story, right?" Tobias shook his head and leaned down to get another drink. "Let's go find a place to sit, it's time you learned about the IRS's biggest failure." Tobias leaned up from the fountain and looked at Trollum, "we can't talk about it here?" Trollum shot him a look and jerked his head towards an adjacent hallway. Soon the two agents found themselves in an empty presentation room.

"Ok Tobias," Trollum began, "As you know the IRS was

created in 1862 under President Lincoln. However, what you and the rest of the world don't know is that the first IRS agents weren't too focused on taxation. They were soldiers in a war of attrition. The American Civil war was at its height when the first IRS agents hit the supernatural playing field with their allies. The Confederacy was not prepared. So in a desperate attempt, a confederate representative was tasked with making a deal with the fairy kingdoms of Summer and Dark." Trollum paused her and grimaced.

"It didn't go well. The Confederate and Fairy representatives met in Atlanta to discuss terms, but our agents were already there. A brutal fight ensued between the three parties. The fairies representative was a prince of summer named Fair-shade. He was the first born child of Mab and Oberon. As the battle

progressed the Confederate representative fled and the Prince and an agent called Abernathy faced each other in single combat. Fair-shade may have been fey but Abernathy was a master sorcerer. Their battle laid waste to the fifth ward of Atlanta." Tobias shifted uncomfortably, he could sense the story was about to turn dark.

"Fair-shade had Abernathy on the ropes. So with a last burst of strength Abernathy stabbed the prince in the chest with a cold iron fire poker. In case you didn't know, cold iron is like solid acid to faries. It burns through their skin like fire. The stronger the fairy the slower and more painful the burn." Tobias leaned forward intrigued, Trollum coughed and continued. "Abernathy plunged the poker deep into the prince's chest. Then with a push of extreme will, fueled by his own life force, he caused the poker to shatter within the Princes' chest. The Prince burned, alive, for three days before he finally died. By that time Abernathy had hunted down and killed the Confederate negotiator, choking him to death in a bathroom in Texas." Trollum frowned as he thought over his words.

"After the death of her son, Mab went insane. The kingdom of winter went from cold and just too harsh and cruel overnight. She waged her own war against the Confederate states, it was a terrible sight. Men, women, and children froze to death in their beds. Ogers raped and pillaged through the south. The Earlking himself led a wild hunt which destroyed the majority of Louisiana. In a last-ditch effort the south surrendered to the North and begged for someone to save them. Abraham Lincoln himself attended the planning meeting. He approved a weregild, blood money, to be paid to the Fey. And, he offered a sacrifice to stop the bloodshed. Himself." Tobias's eyes grew wide with realization.

"Then a few nights after the agreements were signed. Lincoln traveled to the Ford theater and died for his country. An actor was framed and later executed for the crime. Since then we have been at peace with the Fairy kingdoms. But, it is only because of the willingness of Oberon and his children. If Mab had her way she would plunge us into an eternal winter. You were the first human in over two hundred years to not only stand up to her but to confront her directly. That makes you a target." Tobias swallowed audibly.

"well," Trollum said placing a hand on Tobias's calf. "Could be worse right? At least she can't kill you outright." Tobias shook his head and stood up. "Right." Trollum looked at Tobias and smiled. "Don't worry, we will all keep you safe. After all, you are family." Tobias smiled softly and nodded. "Let's go get ourselves some accountants." Trollum chuckled and started heading for the door. Tobias followed Trollum and began to think about what he would do.

They walked through the halls of the convention center for what seemed like an eternity before they came to a large wooden door. "Reception hall 2-B," Tobias read aloud from the piece of paper taped to the door. "8:00 mixer, 9:00 panel on 'teamwork', 10:00 'Vampires and you, the glass ceiling for the undead." Tobias looked at Trollum who shrugged and then he continued. "and at 12:00 'panel of the world's best dictators including Stalin and Steve Jobs." Tobias glanced down at his watch, it said the time was 7:45. "Fifteen minutes till the mixer," he said as he turned toward Trollum. Trollum looked up at him and then down at the map they had received when they had registered. "Well," he said idly, "want to go look at our booth in the main hall". Tobias shrugged and the started to head towards the main hall.

The hall in question was called '1-A' also it was known as 'the thunder dome'. Inside all manner of personnel from different companies bustled about getting their booths set up. Tobias and Trollum wandered along, with Tobias stopping now and then to point out different companies. "There are Microsoft and Apple, they are probably here looking for tech support guys. Oh! And look the vampire families have a booth here as well!" They walked by one particularly haggard group of men and women who were busy building a booth, Trollum grimaced and shied away from them. "Who are they?", Tobias asked. "Electronic Arts and Blizzards public relations and social media department. They accidentally hired a troll two years ago and they still haven't recovered." As he said this a horribly misshapen creature shuffled towards the EA/Blizzard booth. "Let's go team!" it cried raising its disgustingly grotesque head. Pus drained from its eye sockets and it smelled like a dead fish, "Let's not forget our motto guys! SAY IT WITH ME". The beast pumped its right arm as it chanted. "EA! The only thing shittier than us is our DRM!" Trollum shuddered and started to walk faster as they passed the booth.

Soon they found themselves standing before a booth. "We...don't have to build it?" Tobias asked with a raised eyebrow. "Nope!" Trollum said brightly, "We are the most favored company in this whole thing. We will field more applications in an hour than most of these guys will in the whole weekend." Trollum grabbed a bottle of water off of the booth's table and twisted the cap off. "So we essentially get treated like kings. A lot of these demons and monsters are hopeful about working with us because of the Director." Tobias balked at this, "The director? As in our Director?" Trollum nodded, "yup, he is famous around here as the first interdimensional horror to ever hold a high ranking position. Shoot, he was the first shoggoth to ever learn the human tongue." Tobias looked at him with raised eyebrows, "Shoggoth?" Trollum tapped his pen to his lips before replying. "A shoggoth is a beast of pure nightmare. Formed from the primordial ooze of the elder gods and of the dread lords (something I will explain later)." "Oh," said Tobias. Trollum shrugged, "Still better than working for some humans though." Tobias had to bite back a smart assed reply because the loudspeakers suddenly squealed with an inhuman sound. "Oops," Trollum said starting towards the door, "we are late for the mixer."

Tobias and Trolum sprinted through the halls towards the mixer. However, when they finally got there the door was already shut. In front of it stood a large demon with curving rams horns. He wore a black suit with a red tie. In his red claws, he held a battle axe that was easy twice the size of an average man. As they approached he squared his shoulders and growled low and menacingly. "No entry permitted after the party starts." Tobias and Trollum skidded to a stop and stared up at the creatures giant bulk. He glared down at them with fire filled eyes and snarled.

Behind him and through the door came the muted sounds of classical music and laughter. Tobias coughed loudly and grinned at the demon, "But you see sir, we are the honored guests! The IRS." The giant demon snorted and rolled his eyes. " So? Lucifer may care who you are. But a lot of us older gents don't." The demon leaned down until he was nose to snout with Tobias. "Now, piss off." Tobias held his hands up in a surrendering gesture and backed away. "Actually they are with me Aziraphel." Came a smooth and silky voice from behind him.

Tobias turned and found himself face to face with a creature of unimaginable beauty. Her body curved like an elegant river flowing with sensuality. Her lips were perfectly formed around her teeth when she smiled. And her white hair seemed to sway in an invisible wind. "Mistress Death," Aziraphel grunted through his permanent grimace. "Of course if they are with a horseman... err person. Then they are welcomed, guests." Death smiled and beckoned Tobias and Trollum to follow her as the doors opened. And Tobias and Trollum followed death willingly.

The party was an elegant affair filled with men, women and eldritch horrors of every kind and shape. The boys followed death as she led them through the crowd to one of the many tables spread throughout the room. Tobias paused as they passed the stage, "Is that?" Death slightly turned her head and smiled softly. "Yes indeed, Wolfgang and Sinatra make a good team together don't you think?" Then she continued on, beckoning the boys to follow. They shifted through the crowd like water flowing around rocks, until they finally reached their destination.

They approached a table and death gestured to three empty chairs, "come sit with us. I would have words with the champions of the IRS." Trollum blushed as he sat down, Now I don't know about being champions...but sure." He said as he glanced into the face of death. At the table sat three other people. "Allow me to introduce my brothers," Death said with a wave of her hand. "This is war," she gestured towards a fat man with a large gut and an enormous red beard. "Always a pleasure to see members of the US government." War smiled toothily and leaned forward and whispered, "You know your bosses are my best customers." Death giggled and pointed across the table, "This is Famine," A tall thin man with gaunt features and hollowed eyes smiled and inclined his head. "He doesn't speak much. Modernization has done quite a bit to weaken him."

"And this," She said her hand landing on the shoulder of her neighbor. "Is pestilence, I apologize if he doesn't seem to be paying attention. He is authoring a new paper on how vaccination causes Homosexuality." Tobias looked at Pestilence, "They cause homosexuality?" "No," replied Pestilence sharply," But somewhere some idiot will believe that they do. And then that's one more person I can screw with." His fingers fell sharp and fast on the laptop in front of him and he grimaced. "Wi-fi is awful in Hell."

Before pestilence could continue his thought the music changed to a heavy metal rendition of Mozarts 5th symphony. "Tobias," a soft voice whispered
 in Tobias's head. He turned to look around the room to see who spoken. His eyes flitted over Death and then stopped when he noticed that she was staring at him nonchalantly. "Good, you can hear me," Deaths voice slid through his mind like smoke. "We need to talk."

"That's never good, "Tobias thought. "Indeed", Death replied. "It is, however necessary." She leaned forward and studied a point on the walk behind him. "Tobias," Her voice said, splitting the silence in his own head. "Soon you will need to make a choice." Tobias glanced at Tollum to see if he noticed what was going on. He was deep in conversation with war about the Civil War. "What do you mean," Tobias thought back. "Soon, my dear sweet Tobias. You will be forced to choose between what is right and saving a friend." Death leaned back and regarded Tobias through half-closed lids, "And when that time comes I will be there. Waiting in the shadows for you to make your bargain. Just make sure you have something truly worthy." Tobias nodded slowly as an image of death looming over him as a vulture burst into his mind.

Tobias sighed and held his glass up to death and grinned. "But I won't die tonight, right?" He said slowly. Death grinned beautifully, "No, my dear. Not tonight, though I do believe you are about to have a guest who wants to talk." Tobias arched an eyebrow at her as she got up to leave. He was about to follow her when he felt a large hand land on his shoulder. "Mister Tobias," came a thick and gravelly voice. "May I have a word?" Tobias nodded without looking and gestured towards the chair across from him. The owner of the gravelly voice came around and slowly moved into his field of vision.

It looked like a grotesque form of a man. Its limbs were too long and gangly and its jaw hung down like a putrid orifice. Its hands were gnarled and green like the rest of its body, and they landed on the table with a heavy thud. It grinned at him in a gap toothed way and slid a long purple tongue across its already moist lips. "A pleasure to meet you mister Tobias, I am Daniel I. Steal , CEO of Delta Airlines" Tobias looked at the disgustingly obese and moist creature disinterestedly. "So?" The CEO coughed and leaned forward, "We have been led to understand you dislike our company?" Tobias looked at him and grimaced as his scent reached his nose. "Yes, I do." The CEO grinned, "Well what would you say we could do better?" Tobias smiled sarcastically, "Not exist? Sell your planes to Southwest airlines and give up? Go back to your old job?" The creature frowned and leaned back, "Southwest doesn't offer the same service as us. And I feel like you are really just complaining over nothing." Tobias stood up to leave and leaned over the filthy monstrosity. "You're right, Southwest actually offers customer service. You and your staff are just too inhuman for that." Tobias turned smartly on his heel and walked away with a smug grin. He ignored the indignant huffing and puffing of the CEO behind him.

Tobias headed for the bar and had just ordered a cosmopolitan when two men slid up between him. He first looked at one then at the other, they were twins. "Can I help you?" He asked as he picked his drink up. "We would like to discuss you making a campaign contribution." The one on the left said. "No thanks I don't support the..." Tobias glanced at the elephant pin on the man's shirt. "Republican party," He said with a slow shiver. "Well then how about me," the other man said as he brandished his donkey shaped pin. "Ehhhhhhhh, no.... Are the two of you related?" The two men looked at each other and smiled, "We are twins! Each of us are the exact same, we just steal from different people." Tobias was about to ask another question when he felt a cold presence from his left hand side. "Both of you, piss off."

Tobias turned to look at the newcomer and was shocked by his normalcy. He was a man of middle height who had dark hair and black circles under his eyes. Tobias held his hand out on reflex, "Tobias Schmit, IRS." The man grasped

Tobias's hand and smiled, "Lucifer, prince of darkness." Tobias jerked his hand backed and nearly fell over. :Lucifer coolly grabbed Tobias by the front of his shirt and held him up. "It's alright, I'm not here to make deals tonight. Just wanted to talk to the newest recruit for the IRS. I heard about your run in with my sister in law a few months back." Tobias looked at the fallen angel blankly, "excuse me?" Lucifer rolled his eyes and mouthed the word , "Mab" "You two are related?" Tobias said in shock. "Yeah and can you believe she is the bigger bitch?" Lucifer smirked as he said this and nodded to the bartender.

They sat in silence for a moment. "I figured there would be more satanists here..." Tobias said non-chalantly. "Bah! I hate satanists." Lucifer replied as he leaded against the bar and picked up his drink. "They are so overly dramatic and annoying. I can't stand it, it is like dealing with five-year-olds every time they die. They take the whole thing too seriously and are just a bother." Tobias mulled this over for a bit and then smiled, "So like evangelicals?" Lucifer let out a bark of laughter and then nodded his head vigorously. "Pretty much. People tend to use religion like a drug. They become addicted to it and then they are just embarrassing. Like groupies backstage at a concert." Tobias took a sip of his drink and held his hand out, "well it was fun meeting you, but I better go find Trollum if we are going to be ready for tomorrow." Lucifer shook his hand and pulled him in close, "watch out for Mab. I may be like a prowling lion but she is like a snake. At least you will be able to see me coming, her not so much."

The rest of the night was a blur to Tobias and by the next morning, he and Trollum were sitting inside the booth fielding applications left and right. "Red pen," Tobias said over his shoulder while he held his hand out. Trollum handed him a red pen and grabbed an 'approved' stamp. He slammed it down onto the paper angrily and sighed. "Honestly I had hoped for more of a vacation this time," Trollum muttered loudly. Tobias looked around and noticed that the crowd at the fair had thinned out. As a matter of fact, they were only a few minutes away from closing time. He glanced at Trollum and shrugged, "Take the rest of the day off buddy. I can handle the rest here, after all, you deserve it." Trollum looked at Tobias and nodded, a grateful smile spreading across his face. "Thanks," He stood up and stretched, "I will see you at the hotel then?" Tobias smiled and nodded. "Count on it."

An hour later Tobias was finishing the last piece of paperwork when a young man walked up to him. "Sir?" Tobias didn't look up and muttered, "We aren't taking any applications now, sorry." A tittering laugh escaped the boy's lips and made Tobias look up. He was a young boy, no more than twelve, he had horns growing from just above his ears and he wore jeans and a graphic t-shirt. "Oh," Tobias said straightening up and massaging the palm of his hand between his thumb and forefinger. "I'm sorry I thought you were an applicant." The young boy shook his head and held out an envelope, "Someone gave these to me and told me to give them to you." Tobias took the envelope cautiously and looked at the boy. "That's it?" he asked. "Ah no," he shuffled his feet and looked around. "He also wanted me to deliver a message." Tobias raised an eyebrow and gestured for the boy to continue. "He said for me to tell you," the boy began.

"You dine under the sword of Damocles. You sleep upon a bed of vipers. Death will seek you and she shall not find you. And when your soul shall cry out even the shadows shall turn their backs to your pain."

Tobias shivered as the boy finished. He stared for a minute as he tried to make sense of the situation and then nodded. "Thank you," he said. The boy smiled and nodded in return then turned and left. Tobias sat down and pulled out the envelope he had been given and ripped it open. Four pictures slid out onto the table. Each one seemed to have been taken through a long range scope.

The first picture showed Trollum talking with Rapunzel and Cat outside The Pub. He was holding a small bundle in his arms and smiling down at it. The crosshairs of the picture landed directly on the bundle. The second picture was of Natalie and the Babayaga. They were both ordering coffee at a Starbucks. The scar on her calf shone brightly in the picture. The crosshairs were planted directly in her chest. The third picture showed Tom and his boyfriend at a farmers market. The crosshairs were on the back of Tom's head. The final pictures made Tobias swear out loud. It was him and Frost. She was kissing him and the crosshairs laid right across her head, the 'x' sitting squarely on the base of her skull.

A small note was mixed in among the pictures. It was written on stationery that was cold even in Hell. Steam rose from the card in black cold lines as he read the typed words on its face. "One will fall, One will Die, Another will suffer And the last is a lie. -Mab" He stared at the card dumbfounded and then he threw it down onto the table. And he silently thought over what his decision should be. Finally, after hours of contemplation, he came to a conclusion. He sneered as he glared at the card and hissed a single word.

"No."

(SUMMER)
Inter Chapter Exposition

Tobias Takes Frost to a Mall to discuss their relationship
&
Trollum has to go to court to testify for the director

IRS

CASE FILE
PROPERTY OF THE UNITED STATES OF AMERICA
DESIGNATED : Security clearance level Omega

Tobias looked at the illuminated sign above their heads and pondered the many choices it held. "I think I want a number 3," Trollum said as he did the same. Tobias glanced down at his friend and smiled. They were both standin ing the Mc Donalds fastfood restraunt on the corner of the street next to the IRS compound. It was a Saturday and if was getting close to the end of summer. It was suppposed to be their day off but the two agents each had a special case to do.

"So what is it you have to do again?" Tobias asked as he began to think about whether or not he wanted fries. "Ehhh Natalie is having me come and testify on something at the court house. Apparently someone in our department is in trouble and they need a character witness." Tobias nodded slowly and decided he did not want fries with his order. "What about you?" Trollum said as they shuffled foward in the line of people waiting to order food. "I am meeting Frost at the mall of america, we need to talk about the issues with her mother." Trollum sighed and ran a hand through his hair. He wasn't wearing his usual office attire and as such he didn't have a hat. In point of factr, he was wearing a old Dropkick murphys t-shirt and a pair of tattered and well worn jeans. Tobias of course was wearing his trade mark white shirt (with the sleeves rolled up) and tan pants. His brown hair seemed to shine in the sun and his moustache was combed and waxed into perfection.

They advanced again and were only one person away from ordering. "You know this is a serious situation." Trollum said as he examined his finger nails. "Yeah, I know. Just bathers the hell out of me. I figured she should know what her mom said and at least be prepared if something happpens. Did you tell Cat and Tom and Hiroshi about all this?" Trollum sighed and nodded, "yeah Hiroshi is 'visiting' his fmaily in Japan for a while and Aki went with him. Tom said that she wont try anything against him since leprechauns are her husbands subjects. And Cat is staying at one of the Royal vineyards in California. You know you missed a hell of a wedding." Tobias shrugged and gestured at his side, "I really didn't want to get stabbed again." Trollum snorted and jerked his head foward as the last person stepped out of line.

The two agents walked fowards and were greeted by a smiling and acne ridden face of the cashier. She looked at them and smiled, "Welcome to McDonalds! Can I get you a Mcshake or a Mcburger? Or maybe you would like to try our Mcribs or Mcpizzas? McYUMMY!" As she said this she leaned up on the counter and batted her eyelashes. Tobias and Trollum looked at each other and grimaced, " Lets get the Mchell out of here." Tobias said as he backed away. "Yeah, I lost my Mcappitite. Imma get a sub." The two agents walked out onto the sidewalk and shurgged at each other, "Later!" and then they went their seperate ways.

Tobias was walking into the mall of America when Frost suddenly appeared at his side. "Helllllo lover!" Frost said as she wrapped her hands around his arm making him jump. "Dammnit Frost," Tobias excalimed (but without any real anger to his voice). She leaned up and kissed his cheek as they entered the mal and began to walk. "So what is it that my man wants to talk to me about?" Tobias sighed and gestured towards the path to the food court, "lets walk while we talk and then we can eat. I kinda missed out on lunch."

Frost let out a trilling laugh and tightened her grip on his arm.

As they walked Tobias filled her in on the situation. When he reached the point about the message he had recieved she muttered a curse and shook her head. "Yeah that sounds like her. She really really hates you." Tobias shrugged, "I don't really care if she hates me, but she has threatend everyone I care about. Including you." Frost smiled darkly, "well you don't have to worry about me. I can handle myself." Tobias laughed and touched her cheek with the tips of his fingers. "I worry because I care honey, not because I think you are incapable." Frost touched his hand with hers and smiled. "Thank you, I lov-" She stopped mid sentence and looked over his shoulder frowning. "Did you see that?"

Tobias turned around as she pointed and looked across the walkway. She was pointing at a piar of faceless mannequins in a shop window. "No?" he said and he would have said more but then he saw the smallest hint of movement. Together they walked over to the shop window and peered at the mannequins. "Did that mannequin just move?" Frost said as she stared at it in a mixture of horror and panic. Tobias smiled and shook his head. "Must have been our imagina-" The mannequin choose that exact moment to break through the glass and lunge for Tobias's throat.

Tobias side stepped and pushed Frost away as the Mannequin moved towards him. It fell to the ground with a hollow thud and then its joints began to twist and pop and the mannequin righted itself and stood up. Then with a steady gate is started towards Tobias. Its featurless face gave off the sickening feeling that it was smiling at him. Tobias started to back up slowly until his back hit the edge of the malls Cinnabon (because all malls have a Cinnabon) .The mannequin lurched towards him slowly and Tobias reached back for a weapon any weapon. The mannequin was almost upon him when his hands found purchase and he grabbed a cinnamon role. But not just any cinnamon roll, this was a Cinnabo cinnamon roll. And it was one that had been sitting out for less than an hour so it was hard as a piece of granit, with twice the density.

Tobias let out a battle roar and lunged at the

Mannequin with his bread of death. The mannequin stumbled backwards as Tobias brough the cinnamon roll down onto its head caving the cheap plastic in on itself. He grasped the pastry in a two handed hold and benga to ram it down onto the creatures head again and again. He only stopped once frost ran over and pulled him away from the cinnamony massaccer. That was when he heard the singing.

"A fiddle dee dee and piddle dee who!" A voice like a bell sang. Then there was a flash of light and before him and Frost stood a woman in a blue robe. Frost spit onto the ground and rolled up her sleeves. The woman had a face lined with wrinkles but they were all in the wrong place for someone who should have smiled. Instead they framed her face and made her look crule and miserable. "Tee Fiddle dee HEE! Princess Frost you need to be careful! Going on a date is a bad thing and being in-" "Shut the HELL UP!" screamed Frost as she stalked towards the woman. "I told you once and I told you twice you sycophantic psycho! I DON'T NEED A FAIRY GODMOTHER!" The older female fairy waved her hand through the air. "Of course you do dearie. You are persecuted by an evil mother and you need a man to come save you. Until them you need me." Frost's hand landed on the handles for a mall kiosk and she began to drag the kios behind her.

"I do not need a man to save me. Yes I am a woman." AS she stepped the concrete under her feet began to crack. "I am a princess and yes I have a bitch of a mother. But, I am a grown woman and I can deal with my own shit! I AM NOT SOME WEAK FRILLY SKIRT WEARING PEARL CLUTCHING HOUSE WIFE FROM THE FIFTIES!" She planted her feet and with a roar swung the mall kiosk over her head and brought it crashing down on the fairy god mothers head. The kiosk splintered into a thousand pieces and the fairy godmother let out a death gurggle as she was crushed by millions of cheap cellphones and crappy makeup.

"Frost are yo-" Tobias stopped speaking when Frost held a finger out to make him be quiet. Then she looked over at a man who was sitting at a table a few feet away. "Tell my mother she can go drown for all I care. He is my man and I am not letting him go. I might even marry him." Tobias's eyebrows rocketed to the tob of his forhead as she said this. The man stood up and nodded at him and then at her and dissappeared in a flash.

Frost suanterer over to Tobias and picked him up off the ground and smiled approvingly. Then she leaned in and kissed him deeply and passionatly. "Tobias," she said as she pulled back and bit her lip. "Y-yeah" Tobias said, trying to catch his breath. "This counts as dates two and three. Lets go back to your place for the night." Tobias stared dumbfounded and then nodded and grinned. With that they left the Mall of America hand in hand, and heart in heart.

Trollum loved sub style sandwiches. He loved the taste of deli meats and the texture as he bit into them. Which was why he was arguiong with a security guard outside of a court house at 3 in the afternoon. "Look can I leave the sandwich with you?" Trollum pleaded as he took another bite. "No sir I do not hold food. You either finish it out here or you throw it away." Trollum was about to come up with a smart reply when Natalie came through the door, her eyes were enraged and she stared at him in shock. "YOU WERE SUPPOSED TO BE ON THE STAND THIRTY MINUTES AGO!" Trollum shrugged and poiinted at his sandwich, "I'm hungry!" Natalie stalked over and ripped the sandwich from his hands and tossed it. "Hey!" Trollum screamed as he watched the sandwich sail through the air and hit a kid on a bike. Natalie grabbed his arm and dragged him through security and into the court room.

The court room was dark and must y and filled with people from all different walks of life. On one side of the room sat a lawyer and a man in a body cast. On the other sat the director and a older woman who was knitting. "hello Natalie dear, is this the man who will help my Harold?" Natalie smiled warmly and nodded, "yes misses director, this is Trollum." Trollum stared at the woman and then at the director. One of the directors eyes looked at him and its mouths grinned , "TROLLUM. EXCELLENT, MAYBE YOU CAN HELP CLEAR UP THIS MESS." Trollum flinched as the words flew through his brain. "Harold dear," the older lady said as she turned her self around. "Perhaps you should try speaking with your voice. The young man is obviously in pain." One of the mouths rolled around to face them and a smooth bassonet voice came from it. "Of course darling. How is this Trollum? Better?" Tollum stared at the mouth and then at the old woman " HAROLD?!" Trollum squeeaked in a high picthed voice.

"Yes?" the Director said. "You are named Harold and you never told us?" Trollum said in a hushed whisper. The old woman smacked at a tentecal that was laying on her thigh, "Harold! How could you not tell them your name? Don't tell me you havent been going by the 'director' this whole time?" The director/Harold shuddered and it seemed to take on an air of bashfullness, "Now Maude, I have to retain the title. It is expected of a man in my position." Maude looke dup at the director and grinned, "I suppose you are right dear. Oh! It looks like they are about to start." The judge walked out onto the stage and called the Director forward. His face was a mask of complete and totel indifference as the director approached the stand.

"Mister Harold Highsmith." The judge began. "Will you please explain to the whole court why we are here today?" The director jiggled nervously and began to speak. "Well it all started when my wife came home and told me about how she thought a dad was beating one of her students. You see she teaches kindergarten your honor and she had noticed some bruises on a boy named James. She asked me to look into it to see if she had any cause for concern." The Director noticed the skeptical faces on the people in the court room and looked at the judge. "Can I just show you what I mean?" It asked in an exhasperated tone. The judge leaned foward and waved his hand, "by your leave."

A shock wave flowed through the room and suddenly everyone could see through the eyes of the director and into his past. The Director spoke to a small twisted creature in the backyard of his suburabn home. "I want you to spy on him. Don't do anything else just report what you find." The creature chittered at him in a long dead language and ran off. The scene shifted and showed the director drinking coffee the next morning. His giant bulk was taken clothed in a massive blue bathrobe and his tentecals waved lazily about. The small creature seemed to materialize from the shadows and began to chitter at the Director. "Hmmmmm," the director said once the creature grew silent. "Don't trouble my wife young one. I will handle this... I need you to call this number and have him meet me." A tentecal wrote something down on a scrap of paper and passed it to the creature. It squeeled with delight and dove into the nearest shadow. The director took a sip of his coffee and narrowed his many eyes.

       The next morning the director walked Maude to school and waitied outside in the shade. He silently watched as parents dropped off their kids one at a time. He even smiled at the few children who could see through the viel well enough to see him. Then he saw James, and his elderitch blood began to boil. James had a black eye and his lower lip had a split in it. His father shoved him foward towards the school and belched loudly. He was wearing army fatigues and had a buzz cut. However the fatigues looked wrong on him due to his expansive beer gut. "I fought in Iraq so little shits like you could go to school." He hissed through his teeth as he shoved his son.

"Excuse me sir," the director said as he stepped out from the shade. He had cast a glamor on himself and appeared as a small mousy man with greying hair and large round glasses. He placed a hand on James shoulder and placed him behind himself, "run along son. You don't need to be here for this." James stared at the director in horror, as he could see through his glamour, and ran into the building. "The hell do you think you are doing?" The father asked stepping towards the director. "Stopping something that is truly evil. You sir, are a bad father and an even worse human being." The man stepped foward and poked the director in the chest. His breath stank of old beer and stale ciggaretts. " My son, My property." The director sighed and glanced upward and then back at the man. "I'm giving you one chance before this gets ugly. Apologize and never hit the child again."

James's father let out a loud laugh. "That little brat gets hit because he deserves it. He is a dumb shit just like his mother, but at least he doesn't cry as loud." The directors eyes flashed and he snarled. Making a complex hand gesture and an even more ancient spell the director dropped both the glamour and the viel. "YOU HIT YOUR WIFE?!" Boomed his voice through both the mans soul and his mind. The man crapped himself in fear and fell back against his car screaming. "I SHOULD HIT YOU UNTIL YOU CAN"T STAND!" The director roared like a train through the mans skull, blood began to pour from his ears. "BUT I AM NOT CRUEL OR VIOLENT ANY MORE." The director backed down and the man stood up, his legs quivering in fear. "BUT MY FRIEND IS." And then the man looked up as the sun was blotted out from the sky.

Above him stood such a horror that the very sight drove him mad. It's body was made from billions upon trillions of white wriggling worms. It had twelve rows of multifaceted eyes and two large pincers. Its mouth was an open dark maw and surrounded by razor sharp teeth. It had long wings that stretched out for a footballs length each way. And its hands were as big as busses. "IS THIS THE ASSHOLE HAROLD?" A voice like nails on a chalkboard rang out from its open maw. "YEP" The Director replied. The creature looked down upon the puny man and sneared. "BEHOLD MORTAL I AM YOG SHAGNATOTH LORD OF THE OUTER DARKNESS AND MADNESS. ELDER GOD OF THE THIRD CHAOS AND PRIESTES OF IR'LIEAH! I AM CHAOS INCARNATE BEAR YOUR EYES UPON MY VISAGE AND DISPARE. FOR EVEN THOUGH I AM PURE CHAOS AND ENTROPY. THE BASIS OF ALL EVIL. EVEN I AM DISGUSTED BY YOU." Then the creature leaned down from its towering height and flicked James's father like a paper football.

The judge leaned back as his head cleared and grimaced. "Yeah, I am throwing this case out of court and contacting DCS." The fathers lawyer stood up and started shouting, "He launched my client at super sonic speeds into the side of a gym! We are owed compensat-" He would have said more but suddenly he fell to the ground screaming about flies. The director glided out of the room and wrapped a tentecal around Maude. "Well Trollum," he said as they left. "I suppose I didn't need your help after all." Trollum glanced up at him and then back down at the ground, "why did you help him." The director paused for a moment and then continued on. "Because sometimes it is the action of one individual that changes someones life for the better. A single voice of hope in a void can change things for the better. Trust me I know." And with that Trollum watched as the Director wrapped a tentecal through Maude's arm and they walked off into the sunlight.

(SUMMER-FALL)
CHAPTER 7

CASE #32
IN WHICH TOBIAS GOES ON A ROAD TRIP WITH A PRIEST
AND A RABBI..

IRS

CASE FILE
PROPERTY OF THE UNITED STATES OF AMERICA
DESIGNATED : Security clearance level Omega

Tobias stared at Natalie as she finished speaking. "And that is why we are sending you to Miami." She spread her hands and smiled, "Honestly you should be grateful we aren't sending you with Trollum. The F.A.A.B.Y.M* is almost always held in Jotunhiem. And the only way to get there is to be enter through a gate in a place of permenant winter like northern Alaska." Tobias rolled his eyes in an exasperated gesture and waved a hand at the stacks of paper around him. "Natalie, this is stupid. Why can't you just go yourself? I have paperwork here to do and ontop of that I hate Miami. It's too damn hot." It was Natalies turn to roll her eyes and sigh, "You didn't complain about Hell being hot." Tobias raised a finger and wagged it condesendingly, "That's because Hell is a dry heat. Miami is a hot moist heat and it smells like old people and baergin priced tanning oil."

Natalie frowned and slammed her hand down on her desk, making Tobias jump. "I. Don't. Care." She emphasized each word with another slap on the desk's top. "You need to go and represent the IRS. This is the one meeting every year where all the humans supernatural organizations come together and discuss the problems that are intrinsic to our work. And besides, the Director in it's infinite wisdom." A feeling of conciousness floated through the hall outside past Natalies office door. Moments later they felt more than heard words slam through their head, "DAMN RIGHT I'M INFINITLEY WISE." Natalie leaned against her desk and puffed out a breath before continuing. "He has decided that the IRS should host a panel on issues met by their employees in the field. And you were volunteered as someone who should host it with two memebrs of the other major organizations." Tobias blinked for a second in shock," There are other organizations?"

"Of course," Natalie said with an edge of annoyance. "There is the Order of Saint Moses the Black and the Society of the Golem. The first is a branch of the Catolic Church which focuses on controlling and fighting against the supernatural. The second is a private firm funded by a society of Rabbis within the united states. They focus more on generating peace agreements and trading." Tobias sighed and then started to chuckle nervously. "Well at least they will only be in the room together for a few hours at most right?" A grin that was part grimace seemed to materialize on Natalies face, "Well.... actually you will be car pooling with them down to Miami." Tobias stared in shock. "You have got to be joking!"

"No I am not," Natalie was suddenly serious again. "Ever since you said all that stuff about United back during the Spring they have been refusing to even let us set foot inside their planes. So now you get to drive for fifteen hours straight. In a small cramped car with a rabbi and a priest." Tobias snorted loudly and leaned back, "Sounds like a bad joke. When do we leave then?" "Tommorrow morning, you will meet with them at the enterprise car rentals down the street."

The next morning Tobias woke up with a headache. And he knew that somehow it would only get worse as the day progressed.

"Ah! Here is the Schmendrik!" A tall man cried as Tobias got out of his car in the parking lot of the Enterprise. "See! You goy yutzi I told you that the one thing you can count on the IRS to do is to be on time." He was a tall beareded man who wore a black hat with a wide brim. Long curls of grey hair seemed to sprot from under the hat and hung down on both sides of his face. "Yes yes," came a thick germanic voice from around the corner of the building. Moments later a man walked out dressed in all black except for his white collar. In one hand he held a copy of the Bible and in the other he cupped his still lit cigarette. He was a tall and thin man with gaunt features and a horrible comb over, The priest threw his ciggarette on the ground and sighed before extending his hand. "Alexi Petrov, cheif exorcist with the order of Saint Moses the Black. And this guy is Rabbi Wesman." The rabbi rushed foward and offered his hand to Tobias with a smile. "A pleasure to meet you goy. Shall we get a car? I am getting sunburned by this cockamamie sunshine, much too hot here." Tobias sighed and glanced at his car. For a minute he played with the idea of flipping them the bird and hopping in the car and driving away. Then he waved his hands and gestured towards the doors of the shop, "lead the way."

"Hi! How may I help you sir?" squeaked the

young girl behind the checkout counter as they approached. "Yes I belive we have a car reserved under the name Natalie?" Tobias said as he pulled the paperwork from his jacket. "Ohhhhh I am sorry but we just gave away your rental since you were a minute and a half late." Tobias started to feel his temples throb with an alarming regularity. "Please tell me you are joking?" He pleaded. "Unfortuantly not sir. But, we do have another vehicle avaliable if you are willing to take it" Tobias frowned and leaned on the counter," What is wrong with it?" "Pardon me sir?" said the young woman. "There is always a catch, what is wrong with it?" Tobias said as he glowered, his headache building. "Oh nothing sir, just some bumperstickers that may be a bit off color." Tobias grunted and held his hand out," screw it. Give me the keys." "Wait!," screamed the Rabbi rushing forward. "We need to haggle." "No," Tobias said as he felt his temper start to rise," The IRS paid for the car and we don't haggle." Thr rabbi frowned darkly and stepped back as Tobias started for the parking lot. "Thank you for coming sir!" Yelled the young lady. Tobias flipped her the bird as he walked outside , his head pounding.

The priest, who had satyed outside to smoke saw this and grimcaed. "That's a sin mister Tobias," Tobias rolled his eyes and kept on walking. He skidded to a stop when he saw the bumper stickers and began to curse. "I am pretty cure that language is a mortal sin," The priest grunted as he shouldered past with his suitcase and lit ciggarette. "I can't belive I am agreeing with the Priest, but watch your language ya putz." The rabbi said in a hushed tone as he pushed past him to load his luggage. Tobias looked at both of them in shock and then down at the myriad of offensive bumperstickers and then he sighed and climbed into the drivers seat and started the car. "Where to first?" Alexi asked. "The convenience store and a gas station", Tobias curtly replied. "Why there?" Said rabbi Wesman Tobias had to push his reply through his gritted teeth like liquid through a siv , "because it is convenient."

After two gas station bought dramamine Tobias crawled into the back seat and laid down to close his eyes. The Father Alexi climbed in and started the car while Rabbi Wesman loaded up their destination on his GPS. "Now we wont get lost!" He said with pride. Alexi snorted and shot him a sideways glance, "Bet you could have used that during those forty years of wandering." The rabbi grimaced and coughed, "just drive you un-circumcised piece of drek." The priest chuckled softly as he pulled out of the parking lot, "that's a sin."

Tobias opened one eye and glared at the two of them. Then as they accelerated and the car began to hum softly he began to doze off. His last memory before finally falling asleep was a faint buzzing from his cellphone.

They had just crossed the mason-dixon line when Tobias was shaken awake by a frantic Rabbi Wesman. "Get your ass up goy! We are being pulled over!" Tobias looked out the back of the window groggily as blue and red lights flashed in his face, "So? What's the big deal?" The Rabbi grimaced and looked at the priest whos knuckles were turning white with how hard he was gripping the wheel. "Well, we are in the south. And you are a member of the IRS. I am a jew from New York. And he is a Catholic priest. Oh, and we have a bunch of offensive bumper stick-" A loud rap came from the drivers side window, Alexi rolled it down slowly as a large mustachioed face frowned at him from the other side. "The hell is this?" said the police officer. Who's enormous girth nearly made it impossible for him to look into the car. "Are you on your way somewhere gentlemen? "

"Yes," said the Rabbi. Ignoring Tobias and the Priest, who both shot him a 'shut up' look. "We are headed to a very imprtant inter-faith and goverment meeting. So if you could please let us go that would be great." The officer spit a wad of tobacco on the ground outside the car and frowned. "Normally I would but see one of your bumper stickers really interests me." Tobias let out a groan as the officer smiled. "Now which one of ya'll lilly livered scumbags put a , 'Mike Pence and Donal Trump Americas #1 Gay Couple' sticker on your car." Tobias and Wesman were about to reply when the priest grimaced. "Well if they are they will burn in hell. Along with all the protestants and the sibling lovers." An hour and half later they were all in the county jail on three charges. First was 'obstructin justice' the second was for 'verbally insulting the officer'. The final one was for 'insulting toe officers choice in marriage'.

"Well?" Alexi said as Tobias walked back into the cell from using the phone. "They can't bail us out until tommorrow. So we have to spend the night here, unless either of you has a way to get us out of here." The priest shrugged and seemed to materialize a cigarette out of no where. He muttered a word and the tip of the ciggarette seemed to burst into flame. "Did...did you just do magic?" Tobias half screeched. "Yeah? I'm an exorcist." This response earned a snort from the Rabbi who was busy pulling the foam from the bench coushions in their cell. "Thats what they call it now days eh?" he said as he fashioned a small man from the foam and frowned. "Yes it is." Alexi said defensivly, "And I don't intend to apologize because I use magic to do my job. At least I don't make little idols to do my bidding." "Golems," Wesman muttered. He waved his hand over the small figure and it twitched to life and the Rabbi leaned down and whispered something in what would have been its ear. Then as the figure ran off he turned and faced the priest. "And while we are at it. At least my orginization never agreed with mass murder. Or did you think it was okay for you to kill off other living creatures just because they were magical?" Alexi shifted as a shadow of old shame flashed across his face. "Different times Rabbi."

"I feel like I am missing something." Tobias interjected. Rabbi Wesman coughed and looked at him. "The order of Saint, and I use thet word loosley here belive me, Moses the Black has taken part in what is called cullings. Or the murder of thousands of magical creatures so as to keep their population down." Tobias stared at the priest in shock. Alexi turned and looked at him with sad eyes, "Yes we did that. But you have to understand, they were killing the people who lived in the same area. It was a neccessity to protect human lifes." Tobias sighed and shook his head, "Still I dont fell like thats a good enoug-" "Oh you don't get a say in judgement," rabbi Wesman interjected. "Oh really? And why is that?" Tobias said in a challenging tone. "Because youi refuse to haggle! And that is just as bad!" Thr rabbi nearly screamed as he pointed a finger at Tobias. "NO ITS NOT!" Tobias screamed in reply as he gestured wildly. They would have continued but just then the little figure the rabbi had made returned with the keys for the cell.

They ran through the police station as quietly as they could. "There!," hissed Alexi. "that is the enterance for the garage! Lets go!" They burst through the garage door and found themselves in the center of the police garage. All around them sat large military grade vehicles and vans. "Well shit," Tobias said as he looked around. "Don't worry, I've got this." Alexi muttered as he walked towards a crowd of large black vans. Five minutes later they scared the guard they ploughed through the gate of the police station in a large armored vehicle that said S.W.A.T on the side in big yellow letters.

"Hey goys?" Rabbi Wesman called from the back of the van. "What?" Father Alexi shouted. Tobias rubbed his temples as his head began to pound with an oncoming headache. "Well...ummm" The rabbi Stuck his head up between the seats and glowered. "I think you grabbed a van from a drug bust you mushegener yutz!" "WHAT?!" Tobias screamed as panic began to over take his mind. "What are you talking about?" Alexi said glancing back behind him. He turned around and stared out the front of the vehicle and accelerated slowly.

Tobias placed a hand on Alexis shoulder and leaned in. "Please tell me for the love of God that there isn't pot or something back there." Alexi sighed and shook his head, "It isn't pot." Tobias breathed a sigh of relief and sank down into his seat. "It's cocaine." Alexi muttered as he grimaced. Tobias leaned foward and softly began to bang his head against the vans dashboard and muttered about how all he wanted was some paperwork. They drove for what seemed like hours until they reached the Florida state line. Finally sometime around five in the morning they decided it was time for them to get some dinner.

"Ok," Tobias said as they sat in the back of the van. "We have exactly one day, being today, to get to the conference. So we need to eat quickly and get out as soon as is possible." Rabbi Wesman looked at Alexi and shrugged. Alexi nodded in agreement and then looked out the front window.

"What about that place?" He said pointing across the street from where they had parked. Tobias looked from where he was pointing and then back to them. "You have got to be kidding."

The next thing Tobias knew they were all sitting in a booth in a cheesily decorated restraunt called "the Freaky Leaky Tiki". "So," Tobias said leaning forward. "How do we get rid of all the drugs?" The rabbi looked at the priest and smiled, "I have an idea. Give me until the end of the meal and I will have gotten rid of them goy." Tobias sighed and nodded as he sank into the coushion of the booth and looked at the gaily decorated tiki cup his drink was being served in. Halfway through the meal Rabbi Wesman got up and didn't come back until the very end.

They climbed into the now drug free van and drove torwards Miami. Tobias was laying down in the back when the Rabbi climbed into the back and leaned against the wall and sighed slowly. "Sooooo" Tobias began ," What did you do with the-" "Drugs?" The rabbi answered with a grin. "I dumped them under a box that said lemonade on it." An eruption of laughter came from the front of the cab and Tobias and Wesman looked foward to see Father Alexi leaning against the wheel with tears in his eyes. "What?" The rabbi asked. "That was a lemonade stand," Alexi said between his loud boisterous laughs. "I noticed they werent up to code so I called the police on them because breaking the law is a sin." Tobias and the Rabbi stared at him in shock and horror. "Well, surley nothing bad will happen to the kid right?"

    Tobias was consumed with guilt and it only got worse as they kept dricing along. "You don't think we did anything wrong do you?" He said as he leaned his head against the cool metal wall of the van. "Nah goy," replied wesman as he leaned his head back. "I think it is more the intent of the action than the action itself." Tobias tilted his head towards Alexi, "What do you think priest? Do you think we are going to hell for stealing a swat car and dumping few kilos of drugs in a lemonade stand?" Alexi let out a long winded sigh and flicked his ciggarette out of the drivers side window. "No," Alexi said in a soft tone. "The Rabbi and I may not agree on much but we do agree on this. Intent matters when considering sin. For example, a man may kill his neighbor and not be at fault. But only if it is for a good reason like self defense or to stop a greater evil. Otherwise he is commitiing a sin." Rabbi Wesman nodded sagely as Alexi spoke. The he looked at Tobias and smiled, "What happened is a shame but no more than an accident." Tobias snorted and shot the Rabbi a glare, "Sounds like a lot of desperate rationalizing." Rabbi wesman shrugged and was about to say something when the priest slowed down, "We are taking a break."

Tobias and the Rabbi both raised their eyebrows as the priest pulled into a parking spot. "Where the hell are we?" Tobias said. "The florida welcome center, they serve orange juice here and I am thirsty," Father Alexi replied as he climbed out of the van and began to walk towards the welcome center. "Are you coming Wesman?" Tobias muttered as he headed for the door. "Nah, too much sun. You just come back soon and leave the windows cracked." Tobias nodded and leapt out of the van. Alexi was leaning against the side of the van and eyed him with a grin. "Lets get some orange juice, yeah?"

They walked into the welcome center and quickly found the orange juice. Tobias was admiring a large map of florida while sipping on his glass when he felt a cloth hand land on his shoulder. "So this is where you have been Tobias." Tobias turned around and found himself face to face with a figure clad in a costume which resembled a large cartoon mouse. "Excuse me?" Tobias said as he stared into the souless eyes of the mousey abomonation. "Do you not remember me?" Came the voice again, a shot of ice ran up Tobias's back as he recognized the voice again. He stumbled away from the mouse as it marched towards him. "Thomas."

Thomas, who was still dressed in the cartoon mouse costume advanced slowly. He was half a foot away when a small kid ran up and grabbed at his leg. "I wuv you!" The doe-eyed child said through a mouth full of crooked and missing teeth. He beamed up at Thomas and grinned even wider, "Mommy and daddy are taking me to your theme park! Will I see you there?" The child would have continued but his mother arrived and pried him off Thomas's leg and smiled sheepishly. "I am sorry, you are like his god." Suddenly a voice cried from across the room, "EXCUSE ME?!"

Thomas and the woman slowly turned to find Alexi staring at them. His face was a mask of rage and his ciggarette smouldered in his hand. "Did you just say that ... that thing, is considered a god?" The mother looked from the priest to the cartoon mouse and shrugged. "Well I guess to some people he is?" With a cry the priest launched himself across the room, his ciggarette burting into a ball of flame. A battle roar ripped from deep within his throat as he closed the distance, "BURN THE HERETIC! BURN THE FALSE GOD!" He slid to a stop infront of Thomas and threw a ball of fire squarely into his chest. The cartoon mouse (and false god) costume burst into flames with Thomas inside of it. Much to the happiness of the priest and to the horror of on lookers and the indifference of Tobias.

The priest turned around and raised his hands to the sky screaming, "where is your god now!" Tobias downed the last of his orange juice and nonchalantly grabbed the priests robes and pulled him towards the door. He tepped over Thomas's still burning corpse and grimaced. "Uhhhhh.... Thats all folks?" People stared at him as the door closed behind them, and then he and Alexi broke out into a run for the van. "I am sorry about that back there but heresy is heresy." Alexi said as they pulled onto the interstate. Tobias smiled nonchalantly and shrugged "It's ok, I was always more of a looney toons guy anyway."

Tobias and his compatriots eventually made it to Miami with just hours to spare. As they were checking into their room at the convention centers hotel a familiar cough came from behind them. Tobias turned and foundhimself face to face with Natalie. "What are you doing here Natalie?" Tobias asked slowly. "Oh my flight came in just this morning, I was coming to get you." Tobias stared at her for a minute and then started laughing. "This is no laughing matter Tobias, didn't you get my texts?" Tobias laughed even harder and started to cry, "No. Why is someone dead?" Natalie let out a huff of air and grabbed him by the shoulders.

"No," she sighed as he kept laughing "but Trollum got back yesterday and I have some bad news". "Tobias," he calmed down as he saw the strained expression on her face. "Mab is asking for the fairie to declar war on you. She says that you killed Frost." Tobias felt his heart freeze as she said those words and he stared into her eyes. "Frost is dead?" He said, his voice quivering with fear and mania. "I don't know," Natalie replied. "But whatever is going on you are now at the center of it. We need to come up with a plan."

Natalie grimaced, "We need to talk to a diplomat."

(FALL)
CHAPTER 8

CASE #33
IN WHICH TOBIAS IS FORCED TO PARLAY WITH THE EARLKING.

IRS

CASE FILE
PROPERTY OF THE UNITED STATES OF AMERICA
DESIGNATED : Security clearance level Omega

Diplomats, as it turned out, were truly annoying creatures. To fully understand the being that is a supernatural diplomat one must simply understand the meaning of the term sycophant. That is to say, that a diplomat tends to be a being that schmoozes and generates a general air of being grimy and cowardly. The diplomat that Tobias was meeting with reminded him of a frog. It squatted across form his desk and stared at him unblinkingly. It's skin reflected the lights around it with a moist sheen.

"Mister Schmit," the creature croaked. "You have been accused of murdering the princess known as Frost. As you are no doubt aware this has given Mab causus belli to declare war on you. As of right now her allies have refused to participate in said war." The diplomat paused and belched loudly, its chin inflating and deflating quickly. "As such, I have gained an invitation to the Earlkings hall for his Fall feast. You are to attend and then convince the Earlking to change his mind on helping Mab with her war. If you can convince him to assist us his allies will follow and Mab will be left alone. However, tread carefully, Mab will almost certainly be there."

Tobias stared at the creature sullenly, "Ok."

Trollum, who sat at his desk, looked at him in concern. The diplomat stood up to leave, "Do not fail us mister Schmit. We don not need to go to war over this." He stalked out of the room as Trollum started to stand up. "Tobias," Trollum said as he walked towards his friends desk. "yeah?" Tobias muttered weakly. "Tobias, she will be fine. Mab is crazy but she wouldn't murder her own child." Tobias felt tears start to slide down his cheeks and he turned away from Trollum. " What if you are wrong?" Trollum frowned and looked at the ground. Then he looked back up at Tobias, his eyes were resolute with anger. "Then we do what needs to be done, we end her." Tobias nodded as Trollum said this and then he stood up. "Guess we better see Tom about getting some new clothes then." Trollum's grin grew wide and he beamed at Tobias, "already got it set up. We are going to his house for dinner tonight."

Tom's house was a small Victorian style affair. And, as Tobias noted as they approached, was decorated with gold gilding and a permanent glowing rainbow. "Soooo, a rainbow because of the leprechaun thing or because he is gay?" Trollum snorted at Tobias as he said this and shrugged, "Take your pick I guess." Trollum rapped his knuckles against the front door and waited. He was about to knock again when the door opened up to reveal Dave , Toms boyfriend.

Dave was about three feet tall and had silver wings sprouting from his back. He wore a wife beater over a pair of sweat pants and had a mop of mousy brown hair. His freckles and piercing blue eyes gave him a magical look, as did the fact that he was a pixie. "Trollum! Tobias! I am so glad to see you two. I am sorry about the sweat pants but SOMEBODY forgot to do his part of the laundry this week. And, I absolutely refuse to do his part. He can be such a bitc-" A voice from inside the house screamed, "STOP TALKING SHIT AND LET THEM IN, IT IS FECKING COLDER THAN YOUR MOTHERS HEART OUT THERE!" Dave rolled his eyes and flitted to the side.

Tobias and Trollum walked into the house and admired the gaily decorated living room. It was gay both in the sense that there was a homosexual air about it, and that there was an sense of truly deep happiness. "So Dave? How is the lobbyist lifestyle treating you?" Trollum said as he and Tobias settled down into one of the couches in the living room. "About as well as you would expect. Most politicians expect an LGBTQ activist to be a fairy. But when they see I am an actual FAIRY as well... they tend to have bad reactions." Tobias snickered as he said this and Dave shot him a grin, "I gave a prominent conservative pundit a heart attack!" Dave hovered as he started to re-enact the scene. " I went to visit him and present my case. But when I got in there he threw stuff ant me and got right up in my face. Then he shouted at me and said, ' I don't need any gay fairies in here!' and so I pirouetted and stripped off my glamour Then he began to shit himself in panic. Which honestly I thought was disgusting so I may have enchanted him to poop glittery pink puff balls and piss glitter. I don't think he has been taking it well, he looks rather constipated now."

Dave had a lot of stories and was about to launch into another one when Tom walked into the room. He was wearing a small polka dot apron and had his curly hair tied up in a bun on the back of his head. He grabbed Dave by the shoulder and kissed him on the cheek. Dave made a noise like he was sick and buzzed upwards and away, "Tom?" Tom looked at him and raised an eyebrow, "yeah babe?" Dave dive bombed Tom, forcing him onto the ground and got in his face. "Why the hell haven't you done the laundry yet TOM?!" Tom smiled and wrapped his arms around Dave, "Cause I have been too busy staring at that cute butt of yours." Dave blushed and squirmed to get away.

The two lovers were about to kiss when Tobias let out a firm but polite cough. Tom and Dave both blushed and stood up. "Tobias, Trollum... It is always good to see you two. Dinner is almost ready." Tom waved a hand in the general direction of the next room, "let's eat!" They ate heartily and fully, Tom was an extremely good cook.

After the meal Dave was picking up the plates and silverware as Tom listened to Tobias tell his version of past events. "So let me get this straight," Tom said stirring his wine with his finger. "You stop Mab from assassinating Trollums sister, Then you destroy her alliance with the Elvish kingdoms. On top of this you tear apart a multi-level marketing scheme she was getting a cut from, and you destroy a drug ring that she probably owned. You then had the gall to begin a relationship with her daughter. Also you embarrassed her in front of the elves and killed her only ally in the Greek pantheon of gods?" Tobias shrugged, "I don't mean to it just happens." Tom sighed and sat his wine down, "I am afraid faries don't believe in consequences. Mab hates humans and she hates being embarrassed so I am not surprised you are on her shit list. I just want to know why she would kill Frost, it doesn't make any sense. Unless of course Frost is the traitor." Tobias balked as Tom said this and shook his head, "Impossible, she is nothing like Mab." Tom nodded sagely and then steepled his fingers, "What do you need me for exactly?" Trollum was the one who answered him, "we need you to make Tobias a new suit, he has a date with the Earlking."

"Stop squirming!," Tom shouted as he stuck Tobias with another pin. "Ow! Shit Tom could you maybe avoid sticking me with that thing?" Dave, who was sitting in the corner reading cosmopolitan let out a barking laugh. With his one free hand Tom pointed an accusatory finger, "Shut up you. Or I won't be sticking you with anything for a while." Dave rolled his eyes and sighed. Tobias smiled at their banter and then his thoughts drifted to Frost. "You know she isn't dead," Tom said as he began to sew. "What?" Tom rolled his eyes as Tobias looked at him incredulously. "She isn't dead. Mab wouldn't kill her only viable heir. Besides, killing her would make Oberon turn against her, he loves Frost too much." Tom eyed his craftsmanship closely and then leaned back. "Look before you go to see the Earlking you might talk to Natalie. She used to visit the Earlking a lot when she was out in the field." Tobias looked at his reflection in the mirror and nodded. "Guess I will need to go ahead and pack my crap." This earned a glance from Dave and a muttered, "Need any help doing that?" Which resulted in his receiving a swift smack along the backside of his head from Tom.

The next day Tobias and Trollum were in Natalie's office listening to her talk about the Earlking.

"There are a few things you have to understand about the Earlking." Natalie was silent for a moment as she carefully thought over her next words. "First, the Earlking loves games of skill and challenge. If you get into a situation that is hopeless (as the two of you seem to do everytime we send you into the field) challenge whoever is the antagonizer to a game, the Earlking will force them to accept. Also the Erlkings hall is a separate realm from this one, think like how Odin's mead hall or mount Olympus is separate from the normal world. As such some things may be different, physical or otherwise. Finally the one major thing is to realize this is a fae realm, and that means it is highly dangerous to humans. One wrong slip and you will almost certainly die." Natalie looked at Tobias and Trollum, then she let out a slow sigh. "Honestly I don't feel good sending you into there but it has to be you two. You are the people Mab is trying to declare war on."

Tobias looked at Natalie and frowned, "why aren't you coming?" Natalie looked at Tobias and her expression became hard as stone. "I do not travel into the realms of the Fae. Ever." Tobias arched an eyebrow as he noticed his friends' obvious discomfort. "Why not?" Natalie's hand instinctively shot towards her calf and Tobias noticed, "Is it because of that? Tell us what happened." Natalie stood up and stalked towards the door and slowly shut it. With a shaking hand she turned the lock on the door and then rested her forehead on the surface of the door. "Alright, fine. I will tell you the story about why I don't go into the field." Natalie leaned back and ran her fingers through her hair, " It all starts with the Earlking being a selfish idiot and a vicious bastard."

"I was the premier auditor for the IRS and one of the most successful in the organizations history. I had been tasked with attending a fall ball hosted by the Earlking. My job was to inspect and plot out the course that the Wild Hunt would take that Hallowseve. My partner was an elf named Christina and she had a …bit of a temper." Natalie turned her head to regard Trollum sullenly, "she actually reminded me of you a bit." Trollum squirmed uncomfortably as she continued, " Anyways long story short, the Earlking fancied Christina and tried to claim her as his. Of course this would have worked had she simply been an elf, but she was also a member of the IRS. So she was able to say no without causing an incident, or at least that's what should have happened. Instead, she told the Earlking no and he became enraged. He demanded to know why she refused him and wouldn't let us leave. So she told him that she was engaged to my brother and that she was not interested in fairy." Natalie let out a shudder that seemed to shake her body.

"I still remember how his eyes seemed to become like fire. He swelled to ten times his size, shedding his humanoid form. He had to have been over twelve stories tall and his head was as big as a bus. He looked at us with reptilian eyes and said that only one of us would leave here alive. He claimed that he had been insulted, and that because he was host he deserved recompense." Natalie locked Tobias with a stare and tears welled up in her eyes. "I watched, helpless, as he burned her alive. Even now if I close my eyes I can still hear her screams and smell her burning flesh. Then his guards grabbed me and they beat me and tortured me until I couldn't move...until I couldn't think." Natalie glanced down at the scar on her leg and then back at the two agents.

"When they were through they tossed me through the gate and back into our world. I crawled to the nearest hospital. When they examined me they told me over two months had passed. I lost most of the feeling in my leg due to some of the meat having been eaten directly off my bones. And, I had lost the ability to have children." Tears big and fat slid down Natalie's cheeks and landed on the desk, Tobias leaned forward and placed a hand over hers. "I don't remember everything that happened. But what I do remember I wish I didn't." she stared at the desktop for what seemed an eternity and then looked up. "That's my story. My supervisor retired after I was released from the hospital and recommended me for this job . He then went and challenged the Earlking to a duel for My and Christina's honor. He was the only human to ever win in a game against the Earlking, and he retrieved her remains." Natalie, as she had now recovered somewhat by this point, let out a slow sigh.

"My point is that you need to be careful. The

Earlking is a capricious bastard who will end you for even the slightest insult. But if you do have to fight him..." Natalie reached into a desk drawer and pulled out a collar made of old rope. "Use this and slip it over his head."

Tobias took the collar from Natalie and examined it. Small silver threads ran through the rope. Trollum reached to touch it. When his fingers got within a few inches of the fibers his face twisted into pain and he fell to the ground holding his wrist as if in pain. "What the hell Natalie?! Where the hell did you get a piece of it!?" Trollum screamed as he rolled on the ground, tears forming in his eyes. Natalie smirked and leaned back in her chair. "I have my sources." Tobias looked from Trollum to Natalie in confusion, "Care to explain or should I just sit here and look stupid?" Natalie let out a laugh that was laced with darkness.

"That is a piece of the rope forged by Saint Moses the Black. He was the first human to ever be part of both a supernatural organization and to fight supernatural beings who weren't playing by the rules*. He used that rope to bind creatures of the supernatural world and torture them until they repented of their sins and became peaceful." She looked at Trollum who was busy staring at his hand as if in fear. "When used on a supernatural being it forces them to feel the pain of every single sin they have committed. Be careful with that though because there are only two of them in existence, the catholic church has the other one." Trollum sneered at her and then glanced at the rope in fear.

"I can't believe you didn't warn me, Nat." Trollum said as he stood up.. "Sorry," She replied as remorse washed over her face. "But I needed at least one of you to know how truly powerful it is. And since it doesn't affect humans..." Trollum waved a hand and let out a weary sigh. "So when do we leave for the gate?" Natalie glanced at her watch and grimaced, "Now. But be careful, we have an ally there waiting for you. They are bound by contract to help you but please be careful." Tobias nodded and stood to leave, Natalie reached out and took his hand. His eyes flashed to her face and he stared as tears formed in her eyes. In a croaking silent whisper she said, "If you get a chance, you kill him. If someone kills him for you all the better." Tobias nodded and left.

The gate was in a seedy sports bar in eastern New Hampshire.

Tobias stared down at the sports bar toilet dubiously and nudged a discarded prophylactic wrapper with his foot. "You sure about this?" he said to Trollum as he looked at the brownish yellow water. It smelled bad and looked even worse. "Yeah," Trollum said from the stall next to him. "Just jump in and get it over with... oh god it smells." Tobias flinched as he heard a retching noise come from Trollum's throat. "Ok here it goes," a splash came from Trollums stall. "WHO THE HELL FORGOT TO FLUSH!" Trollum screamed. "You ok?!" Tobias shouted as Trollum began to curse. "I am standing in a toilet and a turd the size of my cat is floating next to me, Tobias! I am most definitely not OK!." Tobias grimaced and started to place one foot into the toilet bowl. After a minute of internally cursing and listening to Trollum curse externally he placed his other foot into the bowl. "Ok what now?" he asked with barely contained nausea. "Now?" Trollum replied, "we flush...ready?" Tobias placed his hand on the handle of the toilet and shouted the affirmative. Then Trollum counted down from three and they flushed themselves.

Tobias had the distinct feeling like he was being pushed through a tunnel that was two sizes too small for him. Then there was an immense pressure and the whole world went black. He looked around in panic at the blackness until he felt like he was being pulled backwards. Then a feeling like he was falling out of water came over him. The sensation that was the exact reverse of falling into a body of water. Then there was light and it was blindingly bright. he felt his head hit the floor with a loud thud just as a cheerful female voice said, "Mister Tobias I presume? Your party has already arrived and has been seated." Tobias pushed himself onto his hands and knees and began to vomit onto the floor. A loud tsk'ing noise came from the direction of the first voice.

He sat up and let out a sickeningly loud croak of pain. Almost immediately he felt a cool glass of liquid being pushed into his hands and a whispering voice said, "Drink this, quickly." Tobias downed the drink in one gulp and his eyes began to become accustomed to the light. A woman with long black hair and Aryan features was holding him up by the shoulder and smiling to the surrounding people. "It's ok everybody!" My friend here just had too much to drink, no need to call a doctor." Then the woman looked at him with a panicked expression, "why the hell are you here? Don't you know after the last... of your kind of human.. that the Earlking banned your people from the hall?" She half screamed and half whispered. Tobias shook his head dumbly and looked around, "Have you seen a little gnome? He would have been wearing a brown fedora with a blue feather." Tobias felt the woman go stiff next to him, "yeah, I know where Trollum is. Come with me." Tobias and the woman shuffled through the crowd and he began to notice that the Earlkings hall resembled one giant sports bar.

The hall was as long as a football field and was just as wide. Booths lined the walls and tables were placed around the area randomly. In the center of the hall there was a long fire pit, a dragon laid across the pit and was slowly being spun on a spit by a large ogre. At the end of the hall a massive throne sat like an ominous monument. The only thing more intimidating than the throne was the creature that sat in it. The Earlking surveyed his domain with a steady eye and a deadly grin that showed off dagger like teeth. His face was something between that of a handsome man and a deadly wolf. Tobias shuddered as he noticed that the Earlkings mouth was surrounded by a thin layer of dried blood. The woman who was leading him seemed to hug closer to Tobias and pushed him towards a nearby booth.

Tobias was shocked to find that Trollum was not only sitting with two men who shared the booth. But that he was also deep in conversation with them. "So you are telling me he banned any human auditors?" Trollum asked, incredulity seeping into this tone. One of the men, an older man with an eye-patch nodded. "Indeed, it was a horrible affair. Made even worse by what happened to those poor girls." The other gentleman, who was almost as old as the first but had a much larger beard, nodded in agreement. "But what could we do? He paid their weregild willingly and by our laws it can never be brought to court again. I can't even write a song or sonnet about it..." Trollum glanced at Tobias and then at the woman. "I see you finally found your way to us then?" Tobias frowned at Trollum, "I was only a second behind you..." Trollum looked at him and raised an eyebrow, "Tobias... I have been here for the better part of three hours." Tobias's eyes grew wide and the woman beside him sniffed. "He was in the between world, humans shouldn't try to travel along Yggdrasil with magical artifacts." Trollum swore, "I forgot about that....THING." The woman shrugged and smiled charmingly, "Don't worry he still has it." Then she looked around the table, "maybe we should introduce ourselves."

The old man with the large beard leaned forward and grinned, "I am Bragi. God of poetry and guardian of the mead of poetry." Tobias looked at him with wide eyes. Then the woman, who had made him sit down and scoot over so she could sit, placed a hand on her chest. "I am Loki, goddess of mischief and magic." Tobias turned to look at the goddess, "I thought you were a man?" Trollum kicked Tobias under the table and shook his head. "It is ok," Loki said looking at

Trollum, "I am many things mister Schmit. I have been a Mare and a Fish. It is no surprise that the ancients got my gender confused so easily. And this is..." She gestured with her hand to the old man with one eye. "Nobody" the old man said gruffly, "Now days in this hall I am nobody." Loki frowned and shook her head. Then she smiled reassuringly at Tobias. "You don't need to worry. I gave my word to Natalie that I would keep you two perfectly safe while you are here. And I fully intend to do so."

Tobias was about to ask what she meant when the sounds of trumpets came from down the hall. "Behold Queen Mab the lady of darkness and ice. Ruler of the land of the dark and wife to Lord Oberon. Long may she reign and short may she grieve!" A voice seemed to cry from all sides. The hall went quiet as Mab began to slowly walk through the hall to the Earlking. As she passed their booth Tobias tried to hide his face. She was wearing a long black mourning robe and had a thin veil over her face. After what seemed like an hour she finally approached the Earlking and kneeled before him.

"Great Earlking," she purred softly. "You who slew Odin and made his hall your own. You who destroyed Nidhogg the dragon and laid waste to the Norse Gods." Tobias noticed the old one-eyed man's hands had curled into fist and that blood was beginning to well up between his fingers. "I come before you to petition that you declare war upon the Auditors. My cause is just as one of their number brutally murdered my daughter, tearing her from my arms and hiding even her body from me. This same man destroyed my businesses and stopped my diplomatic negotiations. He even went so far as to defile my daughter with his filthy touch and his human lips." An indignant grumble came from the creatures in the hall. "The auditors have even insulted you... oh great king. Please help me end their reign of terror."

The Earlking regarded her for a minute and then he began to speak in a voice like ice. "Of course I shall help you queen Mab. Your battle is just and true, and truly they have insulted me and harmed my person as well. But how do you intend to wage war on them may I ask?" Mab smiled and stared unflinchingly into the Earlkings face, "I will raise the world serpent and bring about Ragnarok." The whole hall went silent until the Earlking threw his head back in a howl of laughter. "Excellent!" He crowed loudly as he clapped his hands. The old man frowned darkly and looked at Tobias, "You have to do something." Tobias stared at him and then at the Earlking. " What? Can I do? And what in the hell is the world serpent? And why the hell should I help you> we are on a mission for the IRS not for whoever you are " The old one eyed man's frown deepened and he placed a hand on Tobias's arm, "challenge her claim before she can gain his oath. I have given my oath to not challenge him so I cannot help unless he breaks his oath first." Then he pulled out a manila folder and slid it across the table and rapped his cane on the floor. "And as you can see I have the proper paperwork already done. I submitted it last Thursday and received approval for assistance today." Tobias stared at the old man incredulously and then looked at Trollum. Trollum was obviously deep in thought but he reached over and looked at the file. finally he nodded at Tobias, " It is all in order you have to do it." Lokie leaned over and whispered in his ear, "Trust me, gods though we may be. We keep our bargains."

Tobias sighed and stood up and in a shaking voice cried, "By order of the IRS and as instructed upon my paperwork, I challenge her claim."

The Earlking looked at Tobias in shock and gestured for him to come forward. "I banned your kind Auditor. But as this is a special circumstance I will allow you to speak your challenge." Tobias approached the throne and bowed before the Earlking. "Your highness, first allow me to apologize as I did not know Auditors had been banned from your hall. Secondly, Mab is lying. I have never done anything of that nature to her daughter. As for her other claims, she fails to mention that she broke our laws by operating illegal business in our realm." The Earlking turned his head to regard Mab coldly. "Is this so?" Mab shook her head and smiled, "A false claim my lord. An attempt to sway your beliefs. Human trickery and falseness."

The Earlking cocked his head and snarled, "perhaps you are right queen Mab. But I will not pass judgment until we decide who tells the truth." He considered the two kneeling figures for a moment and then grinned. "A test between the two of you." Mab's eyes shot up and she glared at the Earlking, "My lord thi-" "SILENCE!" The Earlking's voice sounded like a bomb going off and he stood up. "I desire a contest and I will have it. Auditor, name your test and name your champion." Tobias looked up at the Earlking and swallowed loudly. "I name..." A hand fell on his shoulder and he looked up to see Loki standing there. "He names me." The Earlking regarded the Norse god for a moment and frowned, "and you are?" Loki grinned and bowed deeply. "A daughter of Laufey the Jotun my lord. And the auditor declares that his test will be one of true skill. Whoever lasts the most wearing this will win." She held up her hand and displayed the collar of Saint Moses the Black.

A snarl ripped through the Earlkings throat and he leaned down to look at the rope. "You DARE to bring such an object into my hall?" Tobias shied away and looked at the ground, but Loki stood firm and smiled. "Truly my lord I had intended it as a gift unto you. For few are so amazing as you and truly as powerful. Such a magic trinket may be dangerous to mere beasts. But to you it is a bauble that displays your true power." The Earlking stared in shock at Loki. Then a slow grin split his face and he leaned forward to examine the collar, careful not to touch it. "Indeed, very well. This shall be the test then." Loki bowed deeply and glanced at Tobias as she did so. "My Lord you are most wise and gracious. More powerful than any who have walked the earth before or since. Though before this contest begins may I implore that you swear an oath that you shall not be allowed to interfere with the contest in any way?" The Earlking waved a dismissive hand as he continued to stare at the collar. "Yes yes, you have my oath."

Loki turned around and smiled too the crowded hall. "The test has been decided. And an oath freely given may not be broken!" Then a change came over Loki and her face took on a character of darkness. "Shall we begin the contest?"

Mab strolled towards Loki and haughtily held out her hand, "Begin." Loki placed the collar in her hand and Tobias watched as Mab's facial features seemed to tighten.

After the first minute her eyes seemed to become bloodshot and her skin paler. Another minute passed and Mab started to look strained and she called for a chair to sit in. Half way into the third minute she began to weep. By the fourth her tears had become great sobs and blood streamed from the corner of her eyes. Finally she threw the collar across the room and it clattered to the ground. Loki sauntered towards it and picked it up from the ground then turned to face Tobias.

Tobias let out an audible gulp as she approached and held out the collar for him. He wrapped his hands around the fibers and felt, nothing. His mind flashed back to Natalie's office and he remembered how the collar could not affect humans. He smiled at Loki and grasped the collar with two hands and grimaced. "OH THE PAIN," Tobias called out in mock drama as he looked at Mab and grinned darkly. Mab's eyes went wide as she realized he wasn't feeling any pain and she looked to the Earlking. "My lord this is human trickery!" The Earlking glared at her, "Silence woman! The agreement was for each of you to be tested not for the item to affect each of you equally." At this Mab let out a furious screech and glared at

Tobias. Minutes passed by slowly and her rage built every second. Finally he had only thirty seconds before he beat her record. "Earlking!" she screamed, "Do something or I shall!" The Earlking, whose frown had been growing deeper and deeper began to shift, "I cannot interfere woman but you are welcome to do what you can. With my leave." Mab grinned and held out her hand as a sword made of Ice materialized from the ground next to her. She ran towards Tobias with just seconds to spare. She swung the sword and Tobias tried to sidestep her attack. The very tip of the icy blade nicked his hand causing the collar to fall to the ground. The Earlking stood up and began to clap loudly as a grin spread across his face, "well done queen Mab!"

Suddenly a loud shout rang through the hall, "OATH BREAKER!" Tobias looked for the source of the booming voice and his eyes fell on the old man with one eye. The man began to stalk towards the Earlking like an old wolf. "OATH BREAKER, you have forsaken your oath in giving the witch Mab your leave. And so all oaths sworn to you are now forsaken as well." The old man began to shift and change, blue magic flashing and flowing around him in an ethereal mist. A long ragged black cloak seemed to materialize around him and his cane began to grow longer. "You who through trickey and oath stole from me my hall. You who claimed to have killed me and have taken on the guise of Fenris wolf." Mab's eyes grew wide as the man passed them and she began to scramble away in fear. The old man's eye patch fell to the ground and he began to grow in size. His cane had formed into a long spear and two ravens flew from somewhere in the hall to land on his shoulders. Blue light seemed to radiate from his spear and runes glowed faintly along its shaft. The Earlking shrank in his seat until he was smaller than Tobias, his wolf like face shrank as well. It changed into something resembling a mouse. "W-w-we had a deal." The Earlking cried out as he stared at the now giant man. "Indeed, here me now Earlking. I am the all father, Glad-o-war, the hanged god, Ymir Giants Bane, Gallows' Burden, The hooded one ,Geirvaldr . Master of Charms and Runes, Battlefield Walker, the Grey Wanderer." The old man paused here to pick up the Earlking by the throat and lift him up for all to see. "I AM ODIN." Odin then proceeded to grab the lower portion of the Earlking and slowly tear his head form his body. Blood flowed down his massive fists and between his fingers and pooled by his feet. The Earlking let out a sickening screech and blood gurgled between his lip and flowed from his nose and eyes. Wolves seemed to come from the shadows and began to lap at the blood on the ground. Moments later the body of the Earlking fell to the ground with a sickening thud.

Mab stared in horror as her most powerful ally's blood covered the stone floor in front of her and his body was devoured by the great wolves. Then she looked at Tobias, who was also staring in shock. "You killed him," she hissed through gritted teeth. Tobias stared at her incredulously and rolled his eyes. "I didn't kill him you stupid bitch, you broke his oath." Mab let out a scream and rose to attack Tobias. "STOP YOUR ATTACK WOMAN!" Odin's voice rang out through the hall and he slammed the butt of his spear onto the ground. Mab froze in her place and turned to stare at Odin with a face that was as pale as death. "You have desecrated my hall long enough, begone. Lest I reunite you with your ally. Begone witch of betrayal and let it be known you are named oath breaker." Mab cringed away as the word 'oathbreaker' passed Odin's lips. Then she turned and fixed Tobias with a glare that could have killed, "You will die Tobias Schmit. You and everyone you love will rot." Then with an audible pop and a gust of icy cold wind she disappeared from the hall.

"Well that was fun," Loki said as she appeared by Tobias's side. Trollum ran through the crowd and nearly slipped on the blood. His face was flushed red with exertion and he held a dagger in one hand, "Her guards tried to kill me. But Bragi brained them with a harp and ripped the other ones throat out with his teeth." Tobias frowned and turned to Odin. "We will be going now I suppose?" Odin raised a bushy eyebrow and smiled, "No you will not we must speak." Tobias and Trollum stared in shock as Odin returned to his human size and gestured to a nearby table. They sat down and the All father, after demanding his hall be cleared of the Earlkings men and ale be brought, began to speak.

"Mab intends to bring about Ragnarok, the end of all things. Of course we cannot let her do that but my ravens and my spies tell me she has already found the door to Jormungdar's hole. Unfortunately I myself cannot become involved and go there. I cannot interfere with anything that may create Ragnarok lest the fates decide I should die sooner. But, I can tell you where the door to that land is. And I can tell you where the key is." Odin leaned forward and motioned for Tobias and Trollum to do so as well. "The gate is in Norway, buried deep within the ice. Mab has not broken the seal, I would have sensed it, so that means she has made her own gate with the help of some other being. This is of course troublesome but not the issue at hand. You will of course go through the door I built and for that you will need the key that I gave to Merlin as a gift of friendship." Tobias looked at Odin skeptically. "Why do I feel like this is going to get complicated? And what is the world serpent anyways?" Odin grinned and leaned back, "The world serpent is what you would call a COMD a creature of mass destruction. If he is released he will cause earthquakes that will cause mass flooding. He will also cause the very waters of the world to become poisonous and he will kill off all sea life. After he has decimated the human populations ability to fight and survive he will begin to eat and will seek to release his brother Fenrir. Once that happens they will wage war upon the gods of the world and will end this reality as we know it. So don't let that happen... As for the key though. What Merlin did with it I have no idea, but you may ask his descendent."

Tobias and Trollum looked at each other and shrugged. "Who?" Odin's grin grew bigger. "You will find him in the Wizardyry school known as Chickenfeathers. He is a potions teacher there. I would help you but I am bound by ancient laws not to... and I also don't want to do the paperwork" Tobias's head hit the table and he let out a rattling sigh of exasperation as he began to catalogue the mentally required paperwork. Trollum grabbed the nearest drink and downed it in one gulp. Odin let out a barking laugh and stood up to walk back to his throne. "I believe you boys will be going back to school then!" Halfway up the steps he stopped and turned around his eye flashing with dangerous intelligence, "Oh and Tobias?" He said softly in an almost consoling tone. Tobias looked up. "My ravens tell me they saw Frost, she isn't dead. She is being held by her mother at the gate. Oh and I will fill out the form for returning gods on Friday." Tobias stared in shock and smiled as he felt hope bloom in his heart. "Actually sir, you can do that online now." Odin let out another bark of laughter and nodded as Tobias and Trollum left his hall.

(WINTER)
CHAPTER 9

CASE #35
TOBIAS VISITS A SCHOOL FOR WITCHCRAFT AND
WIZARDRY

IRS

CASE FILE
PROPERTY OF THE UNITED STATES OF AMERICA
DESIGNATED : Security clearance level Omega

"Chickenfeathers" was not exactly what Tobias had expected. They had flown into upstate New York via southwest (since Delta Airlines sucks and is evil) and driven for an hour and a half before they saw the turn off for the school. It was marked by a large plywood sign that read, "Chickenfeathers" and below that "Non-magic people not allowed" in bright white lettering. They pulled off the interstate and drove down the road towards what Tobias had expected to be a castle or something from a movie series about magicians. Instead, he was shocked to find a large concrete parking lot and what seemed to be a community colleges campus. Staring out over the campus as he sat in their car Tobias was struck with how much the school looked like any other school. Except that it also looked severely underfunded, even by government standards. By the time they had decided to exit their car and to begin searching the grounds it was seven o'clock in the morning and the students were beginning to arrive.

Trollum climbed out of the car and stretched his arms wide and yawned. "Well it isn't exactly what I was expecting but it could be worse. At least it isn't some giant impractical castle with a lake and stuff." Tobias snorted in laughter as he climbed out of the other side of the car. "Good god, can you imagine what that would be like? You would probably have to take a train and a ferry to get there." Trollum started to laugh as he thought about it. "And," Tobias continued chuckling, "it would probably be haunted as hell." Trollum smiled and shook his head as he picked up his hat and notepad from the back seat, "such a stupid idea."

Trollum was about to make another comment when a small group of students bumped past him, causing him to stumble. "Watch where you are going ass hole!" Trollum shouted at their backs. The tallest student, who had black hair and a bowl-cut, turned around. "Gods in Valhalla! It's a troll!" screamed Tobias and Trollum as they scrambled away. The student was horribly scarred and disfigured. He wore round glasses and was drooling from the corner of his mouth. "Watch your mouth asshole! I am Perry Hatter! I am the bloody chosen one and my father was the best Catcher in this schools history." The horribly disfigured and spoiled boy spit out his words like half-chewed pieces of meat.

"It's not worth it Perry." Said a short redheaded male student who placed his hand on Perry's chest. He had a massive underbite and a malformed eye (as is common with those who are severely inbred). "Shut up Randall! Just because your blood is very pure doesn't mean you have a right to tell the chosen one what to do." Perry screeched at his friend, spittle flying from his disgustingly misshapen maw. "Boys stop fighting!" screamed the female member of their group. She was wearing a sweat shirt and sweat pants. Her brown hair hung is greasy locks around her face and she had an outbreak of acne around the corners of her mouth. "You don't tell me what to do either Mary! You just hang around with us because you have no other friends you know it all!" Mary glared at Perry and flipped him the bird, "I hang out with you because nobody can look at you without throwing up!"

Tobias had heard enough and stepped forward, "look just watch where you kids are going. We may not be magical wizard people but we do work for the government." Randall let out a roar and ran forward to push Tobias in the chest, "get out of here you no magic grumpersnickle!". Tobias easily sidestepped the severely inbred wizard. And Randall ran out into the parking lot and was immediately hit by a Ford F-250 truck with a snake logo on the side. His body went flying and flew into a nearby wood chipper. The wood chipper was, of course, turned on. Randall was immediately turned into a chunky style blood smoothie. Out of the truck leaned a blond-haired boy with slicked-back hair and a hooked nose. "Oh, I am sorry Hatter. Was that your little nasty friend?" Hatter stared at the blond haired boy as he drove off laughing and then he looked at Mary. "Well, shit... let's go get Bagger so her can scrape Randall out of the wood chipper. Stay the hell away from us you.. you...grumpersnickle!" The students began to shuffle away and Trollum stared at Tobias. "What the hell have we gotten into?" Whatever the answer to their questions the two agents knew one thing, It was time to go back to school.

Tobias and Trollum walked through the entrance of Chickenfeathers and almost immediately ran into another student. She was the definition of annoyingly perky. That is to say, she was more hyper than a chihuahua which downed a bottle of anti-depressants and locked itself in an espresso factory. "Hi, THERE! Are you here for the tour?!" Tobias stared at her and then down at Trollum, and then back at her. "No." A frown appeared on her face and she sagged slightly, "Oh... then how may I help you?" Trollum stepped forward and flashed his badge, "just direct us to the potions teacher please?" The student immediately brightened the moment she saw the badge. "OH! You are IRS agents? I always wanted to meet an agent. Is it true what they say? Are you really able to kill anyone you want?" Tobias rolled his eyes as they began to walk and Trollum started to chat with the girl. Tobias walked a little bit behind the two and glanced in the classroom doorways as he passed them.

The first classroom he saw was a man standing in front of a group of young children. "Ok kids you cast this spell and it will make the mean fear monster turn into something funny!" Tobias watched with interest as a kid approached and the professor opened a small box. Out of the box came a man wearing a hockey mask and holding a chainsaw. Tobias watched in horror as the man swung the chain saw through the air and narrowly missed the child. Then he turned and ran to catch up with Trollum.

"How much further?" he shouted as he jogged to catch up. "Oh its down this hallway, maybe two minutes?" The preppy girl replied and then she immediately returned to talking to Trollum. Tobias let out a wheezing breath when he finally caught up and noticed a flash of fire to his right. He turned and looked at the second classroom he saw and screamed. Inside a professor was shooting fire at students with startling accuracy. The students defended themselves quickly and one kicked the professor in the balls. "Ah yes, this is our defense against black magic class." The preppy girl said from Tobias's shoulder. "Is it always this dangerous?" She pursed her lips, "usually yes. But we have been having issues with our accreditation lately so we have been toning it down." Tobias watched as the students began to curb stomp the teacher who kept shooting fire. "Indeed."

Finally, they reached the potion masters office. "Mister Snidley?" the young girl asked. A tall lanky man with long black hair and high cheekbones turned from a whiteboard to look at her. He hunched over and stalked towards her. Then in a nasal and phlegm filled voice said, "My dear how are you? Who are your guests?" Tobias recoiled as the man approached, mainly due to a thick air of sliminess that spread from his body language like a greasy smoke cloud. "Agents from the IRS sir," she said uncomfortably. The young woman backed up and nodded to them and left making no attempt at shutting the door behind her. Tobias and Trollum stared at the professor and he stared at them. "Is she gone?" he hissed in a normal voice. Tobias and Trollum looked at each other then out the door. Tobias closed the door and turned around, "uhhhh yeah?"

The professor stood up and smoothed his hair back. He took a hair tie off his wrist and put his hair up into a ponytail and then produced a packet of moist wipes. With which he proceeded to wipe off eye shadow that had made it seem like he had rings under his eyes. "SO what can I do for you gentlemen?" He said in a completely normal voice. Tobias stared at him in shock and Trollum sputtered, "what the hell is going on?" The potions master smiled warmly, "They expect me to be this creepy old dude. Truth is I am just your average chemistry teacher. But I play the part so the kids don't feel left out or cheated. Most of the faculty are in on the whole bit... I am Nigel by the way!" He extended his hand and Tobias clasped it in his own. "Tobias Schmit and this is agent Trollum. We are with the IRS and we need a certain key?" Nigel's face soured and he frowned. "I am sorry gentlemen but that isn't really possible. You see we are having some accreditation issues and so the headmaster (the senile old fool) decided we should throw a tournament to show off our schools talents. And the prize is an artifact from Merlin." Tobias arched an eyebrow as he said this and gestured with his hand for him to continue. "MY KEY" Nigel said through gritted teeth.

"Well, we really need it," Tobias said as Trollum began to pace around the room. "Well I am sorry, there really isn't much I can do. I don't even have a team for the contest." Trollum stopped pacing and turned to look at Nigel. "You need a team? And the winners get the key?" Nigel looked at Trollum glumly and picked up his coffee mug, it said 'greatest potions master' on it. "Yes and yes. And actually, I just need one person. They don't even have to be a student!" Trollum looked at Tobias and grinned evilly. "Hey, buddy." Tobias looked at him, "yeah" Trollums grin grew wider. "Remember the whole diaper thing?" Tobias's eyes started to grow wide and his face went pale. "Payback time buddy-o-mine."

It turned out that convincing the school board to allow Tobias to submit his name for consideration was the easier part. "OF course a grumpersnickle can compete! As a matter of fact, he can even use his 'technology'." The headmaster said when they approached him with the idea. He

smiled as Tobias filled out his entry form and placed it into a hat. "After all," The headmaster continued. "It isn't like non-magical people can really defeat magic with 'science or anything they can make." The ancient wizard chuckled as he said this.

That night in the dining hall the names were chosen. An ancient and wizened woman named MCGoggles read them aloud. " Perry Hatter will represent house Griffinturnstyle! Liz

Mallard will represent Snakey! Peter Michals will represent Flowerpuff! And, Tobias Schmit will participate independently!" The crowd booed and hissed when Tobias's name came up but soon settled down.

The next day was the first challenge. "The rules are simple! This is the first challenge of three! Enchant these portraits to move!" An ancient witch screamed as she gestured at a line of portraits. The wizards set to their tasks and began chanting spells. Tobias calmly walked back to his car and returned carrying a plasma screen TV. Perry Hatter stopped and stared, drool dripping from his mouth, as Tobias removed the portrait and mounted the TV inside the frame. Then he turned it on and the judges clapped as the picture within the portrait frame began to move and dance.

Perry Hatter screamed as he started towards Tobias. "You cheated! You used technology and not magic!" Tobias smiled at him as the Headmaster stood up and grinned, "I said he could use technology!" Perry backed down but didn't stop fuming. The contestant from Snakey walked up to the TV and poked it with her wand. "How does it work?" Tobias glanced over at her and smiled, "electricity." She raised an eyebrow and looked at the small generator he had brought with him. "What happens when I do this," she said as she shoved her wand into one of the generator's outlets. Immediately her body went rigged and smoke began to rise from her wand. Then she exploded into a million pieces as her wand blew up. Tobias gawked in horror and tried to wipe himself off, as the blood and ichor had settled in a fine mist over the crowd.

Tobias looked at the Headmaster who shrugged nonchalantly. Then he looked at Nigel who was equally panicked. Trollum walked up to him and offered him a roll of paper towels. They were busy wiping themselves off when the announcer screamed, "One down! Tobias Schmit wins this round!" Then the announcer continued, "Will everyone please make their way to the arena for the next activity." Tobias glanced at Trollum as they walked towards the arena and shrugged.

"This activity is simple! Kill the dragon!" screamed the

announcer from behind a two feet thick steel door. The contestants all stood in the center of the boulder filled arena. Perry Hatter had a sword and the Flowerpuff representative had a poisoned pastries (from Cinnabon). Tobias stood in the corner and was making a call on his cellphone. A bell rang and the ground opened up as a twelve-foot tall dragon burst forth and let loose a mighty column of flame from its mouth. The flowerpuff representative ran towards the beast screaming in defiance. The dragon glanced down at the wizard and incinerated him immediately. Then he sniffed the pastry and burned it as well because even evil hates carbs. Tobias sank down behind a nearby boulder and checked the timer on his phone.

Perry Hatter ran towards the dragon with a scream and swung his sword in an arch. It flew through the air and struck the dragon on the leg. And then it broke in half since the skin of the dragon was harder than steel. Perry stared at the broken sword for a minute and then let out a blood-curdling scream. Tobias rolled his eyes and sprinted out from his cover. He barely made it into a dodge roll when the dragon shot a jet of flame at him. He reached out and grabbed Perry by the back of his shirt and dragged him behind a boulder.

"HOW DARE YOU TOUCH ME YOU GRUMPERSNICKLE! I AM THE CHOSEN ONE!" Tobias sighed internally and checked his timer again. "ARE YOU EVEN LISTENING?!" Perry screeched in his ear. Tobias turned to look at him and smiled. "Shut up you twit," Perry screamed in rage and called him a grumpersnickle again. "The hell does that even mean?" Tobias said in exasperation. "Oh... it is like if the n-word and the f-word had a baby and that baby took a dump." Tobias stared at Perry for a second and then grinned, "oh really?" then he clocked him across the jaw with his left fist and leaned back against the boulder. "YOU BROKE MY BLOODY NOSE!" Perry screeched! Tobias was about to respond, but just them his alarm went off and he sunk down behind the boulder.

In the distance a sound could be heard, whump whump whump. A black form appeared in the sky and was heading for the arena. Lyrics of a song drifted through the air, "It ain't me! It ain't me! I ain't no senators son naw!". The loud whump

whump noise increased to a deafening sound as an Apache attack helicopter came over the edge of the arena. The dragon glanced up and roared at this new intruder. Tobias's phone squealed and Bubba's voice came over the line, "Ya clear Tobias?!" Tobias screamed an affirmative and then the Apache helicopters machine guns began to fire. The dragon was drowned in a hailstorm of bullets and fire the likes of which the world had never seen. Two missiles shot out from the wings of the helicopter and vaporized the dragons head.

   Perry Hatter stared wide-eyed as the dragon fell to the ground spraying boiling hot blood across the arena. Then the announcer's voice boomed once again, "Tobias Schmit is the winner!" Then after a pause, the announcer continued, "The tournament will continue tomorrow night at the hedge maze! Also, can Bagger please make it a point to arrive soon and clean this mess up?" Tobias stood up and dusted himself off. Perry grabbed him and stared him in the eye, "You are dead tomorrow." And then he turned and stalked off towards the dormitories. Tobias looked at his phone and grimaced. Trollum walked up behind him and place a hand on his calf muscle, "we need to talk. Nigel and Bubba are waiting at the hotel room."

The hotel room had that faintly smokey smell of old cigarettes and cheap whiskey. Bubba and Nigel sat at a small round table and were chatting about magical technology. Tobias and Trollum walked in just as they finished talking about the possible applications of salamander guts to a bomb. "Well well here comes the champion," Nigel said in a sarcastic tone. Tobias raised an eyebrow and sat down on the lime green bed sheet of the queen bed closest to the door. "What does that mean?" Nigel squinted at him, "you don't get it do you?" Tobias looked at him and shrugged," What is there to get? I win the next round and I get the key, easy peasy." Nigel shook his head and leaned back.

"Not exactly. You saw the sign right?" Tobias nodded, "yeah non-magic people aren't allowed?" Nigel nodded and sighed. "The magical community has really separated themselves from the non-magic community. So much so to the point that some magical people feel that normal humans are lesser beings. Perry Hatter is supposed to be those peoples answer to an ancient prophecy." Tobias stared at Nigel blankly, "And that prophecy is?"

" These are the words which will be spoken by the chosen one 'The needs of the many outweigh the needs of the few or the one, and I sacrifice myself'." Nigel quoted in a solemn tone. Tobias stared at Nigel and broke out into laughter. "What's so funny?" Nigel said in irritation. Trollum started to snicker too and fell against the other bed laughing. Even Bubba started to chortle loudly. Nigel looked around in irritation and then threw his hands up. "I don't like being left out of the conversation!" Tobias waved a hand and put it on Nigel's shoulder, "First how is that a prophecy?! Secondly that's a line from Star Trek!"

Nigel stared in slack-jawed shock at Tobias for a second. "You are kidding me." Tobias shook his head and broke into another fit of laughter. "When did this prophecy come about?" Tobias said through chuckles. "Uhhh around 1982?" Trollum erupted into another fit of laughter, "That's when the movie was released!" Nigel stared at Trollum incredulously, "no it came from an elf who died in a reactor! He told it to one of our best wizards!" Bubba chuckled softly and smiled at Nigel, "Buddy, Spock died in a reactor in the movie." Nigel stared at all three of them and placed his head in his hands with a groan.

"So you are telling me the entire rewarding community has based their sociological and almost religious beliefs on a movie?" Tobias nodded as his laughter subsided. Nigel stared at them in horror and sighed, "it still doesn't matter. You can't win this next round. They will riot if you win." Tobias nodded and then stared thoughtfully at Bubba. "What we need is a way to discourage rioting. And, to display the power of the IRS." Slowly a grin began to form on Bubba's face. "You ain't thinking what I am thinking?" Tobias nodded, a grin forming on his own face.

The next morning the contestants arrived at the hedge maze. Perry was wearing a heavy suit of steel armor. It gleamed in the winter sunlight and he hoisted a sword and wand over his head. "Today we will prove once and for all that wizards are superior in every way!" The crowd cheered and some people even had tears in their eyes. Perry looked around and grinned. "It seems that even the no-magic grumpersnickle won't show up!" As he said this the ground began to shake and the smell of diesel fumes began to fill the air.

A large tank rolled into the stadium, its treads squeaking as it moved along. It was painted bright orange and had a large white 'U' and 'T' emblazoned on the side. It rolled to a stop next to Perry, who was staring at it open-mouthed. The top opened with a creek and Tobias, in his perfectly manicured suit, popped out of the top and

grinned. "Ready?" He said in a chipper voice and tone. Perry began to blather and scream but then the announcer came over the microphone system.

"Welcome to the final challenge ladies and gentlemen! Today our candidates are the chosen one Perry Hatter! With his enchanted armor of glisrendell. And Tobias Schmit with his Sherman tank. Tobias waved to the crowd as they booed and hissed him. Trollum and Nigel waved back though and he felt his mood lighten. "Are the contestants ready?!" the announcer screamed into the microphone. Tobias gave a thumbs up and

Perry Hatter gave a Nazi salute. Then Tobias slid down into the Tank and locked the top.

"The goal is simple! Make it to the center of the maze and touch the key. The winner will keep the key for themselves and will go on our wall of champions! Ready?" Tobias revved the engine and Perry Hatter closed his helmet. "Set!" The tank inched forward and Perry got himself into a running position. "GO!" And the contestants took off.

Tobias rolled through the maze in a straight line using the tank to quickly get to the key. Perry Hatter chased after him in a rage banging against the tank with his sword. In a matter of minutes, the key was in sight and Tobias opened the hatch and quickly grabbed it. "We uhhhhh have a winner?" The announcer said in doubt as the crowd grumbled. Perry hatter backed off and started to scream. "You can't do this! I am the chosen one! I am the one destined to lead our people to greatness! You filthy grumpersnickle!" Tobias had had enough and he swiveled the turret of the tank so that the cannon faced Perry. "Say. That. Again." Tobias said from inside his metal fortress of death. Anger seeping into each word.

Perry Hatter glared at the barrel of the cannon and shoved his face into the end of it. " grumpersnic-", and then Tobias blew his head off with a single shot from the cannon. The explosive round vaporized Perry Hatters head and most of his upper torso. It also dug a two-yard long trench into the ground behind him. The magical crowd stared in shock and many of Perry's supporters slowly lowered their signs and looked ashamed and afraid. "Let this be a warning," Tobias said over the tanks loudspeaker system. "The non-magical people of the united states are not defenseless. And we sure as hell can kill anyone of you if we need to." the crowd grumbled as he said this but dissipated quickly and without incident.

A few minutes later Tobias and Trollum sat on top of the tank looking at the key and talking to Nigel and Bubba. "Well, I guess I don't have a job now," Nigel said. "Nah buddy I am part of a monster hunting outfit and we could use a guy like you. How do you feel about fried balls?" Nigel stared at Bubba as he said this and shrugged. "Guess I could get used to them... I should probably go pack my stuff." Bubba and the agents watched as Nigel walked away, " You will be coming with us right?" Tobias said once Nigel was out of earshot. Bubba nodded his head and looked at the ground, "yeah, I reckon its time I got some payback." He spit onto the ground and grunted as he stood up. "I got shit to do, I'll see you boys in a bit." And He walked off towards the school offices.

Tobias watched Bubba go and then looked at the key. It was small and golden with a runic sigil carved into its handle. "So I guess we go to Norway now?" Tobias said as he slowly turned the key over and over in his hands. "Yep," Trollum muttered. "And either kill Mab or arrest her..." Tobias trailed off at the end as the implications of what he had to do settled on him like a heavy blanket. "Think we can do it?" He said glancing at Trollum. Trollum sighed and looked at his feet.

"We have to, the world is depending on us."

(New Year's Eve)

CHAPTER 10

CASE #35-2
Conclusion

IRS

CASE FILE
PROPERTY OF THE UNITED STATES OF AMERICA
DESIGNATED : Security clearance level Omega

It wasn't the turbulence that woke Tobias up so much as the nightmare he had been having. If he still closed his eyes he could see it, almost like he was still there. Smoke had surrounded him and a giant serpentine shape had loomed in the darkness. Just far enough away to where he could still see it's silhouette. Tobias had watched as the creature in the shadows had surrounded him. He could hear his friends calling out in terror and he could see flashes of light from between the coils of the great snake. He tried to scream but instead, blood had flowed from his mouth. Then just as the snake had reared back to strike, Tobias had woken up in a cold sweat.

Trollum looked over at his friend with concern and sighed. "Tobias, it will be ok." Tobias looked at him and smiled weakly, "I know." At that moment Tom and Hiroshi walked down into the cargo hold of the plane and smiled at them. "How are you holding?" Tom said as he adjusted his armored vest. Tobias shrugged, "About as well as could be expected" Tobias replied with a grin. The four of them and Natalie had left the Air force base in Washington that morning and were flying to coordinates as provided by Odin. Natalie was currently in the cockpit with her brother Bubba and they had been arguing nonstop. That was why the four of them had gone down to the cargo bay, to get some freaking peace and quiet.

Hiroshi sighed as he checked the straps on his backpack and patted the sword hanging from his waist. "It's ok to be nervous Tobias, you would be stupid not to." Tobias nodded his head and let out a tired breath. "I know. I just wish you guys weren't putting yourselves on the line like this." Tom slapped him on the shoulder and laughed, "you don't think we would leave you alone did you? You are part of our family, and we stick together." Tom let his hand fall from Tobias's shoulder and rested it on the butt of the pistol on his hip. "Besides, nobody threatens me and Dave and gets away with it." Hiroshi nodded and gripped the hilt of his sword, "or threatens Akiri."

"So we all have stock in this!" a familiar female voice said from the ladder leading to the cockpit. Natalie stood there dressed in black tactical gear and with a pump action shotgun in her hand. Tobias smiled at her and nodded as he stood up. "Yeah, right." A crackling sound came from the plans PA system and Bubbas thick southern voice filled the cabin. "Ya'll get ready now, were bout' two miles out from the landing zone." Natalie looked at Tobias and arched a perfectly groomed eyebrow. "No armor?" Tobias's hands went to his black suit coat and smoothed it nervously. Then he tightened his tie and grinned grimly. "No, I am an agent of the IRS. I don't wear armor or sneak into places. I go where I please with the full strength of the United States Federal government behind me." Natalie's eyes flashed and she smiled, "The director was right. You do make a good auditor." Tobias smirked as he stalked towards his seat and picked up his bag. "Damn right."

Bubba's voice came over the PA again, "Ya'll buckle up now. We are getting ready to land. Imma turn on some music to soothe nervous minds as we land." The Animals 'house of the rising sun' came over the sound system as they began to strap themselves in for landing. Tobias leaned his head back against the back of his chair and let out a shaky breath. He turned to his left and saw that Hiroshi had a yellowed picture of Akiri in his hand and he was crying softly. Tobias, not being able to bear that turned his head to look at Trollum. Trollum sat there silently and checked his gun. Natalie sat across from him and her face had gone whiter than usual and she seemed like she might start panicking at any time. She jumped as tom laid a hand on her knee and smiled comfortingly. Only Tobias noticed the nervous tapping of his fingers on the butt of his pistol. Tobias let out another sigh and closed his eyes and whispered, "Frost".

Norway was freaking cold. Bubba landed the plane skillfully on the ice-slicked tundra outside a giant gate made of ancient brass. Ice cacked the towering statues that flanked the door. They had to have been at least twenty stories tall and they were only half the size of the door itself. "Shit," Bubba said around the lit cigarette that hung from the corner of his mouth. Trollum looked at Tobias and jerked his head towards the key around his neck. "Well? What do we do now?" Tobias shrugged and walked forward, his black leather shoes sinking into the snow as he motioned for the rest to follow him.

They fanned out in a defensive position as they approached the gate. Trollum approached the door and looked at it in awe and motioned for Hiroshi to come look at it. "You ever seen anything like this?" Hiroshi nodded as he approached and narrowed his eyes. "It's a world gate. A method for traveling along the celestial roads. The tengu and yokai used them during the wars, as you might recall." Trollum spit on the ground and cursed, Tobias, looked from Hiroshi to Trollum, "A world gate?" Hiroshi nodded, "Indeed. The ancient species of the world used to use them to travel to different realms and even to visit their gods. Some called them celestial roads, branches of Yggdrasil, portals to Olympus and many other names." Hiroshi ran a hand along the door and wiped the snow from a collection of runes and symbols. "This one seems to have been a 'true gate'. Essentially it is tied to multiple places instead of just one. I think this might be the centric point for where the Norse worlds are connected. This might even be the-" Trollum's eyes opened wide and he touched the door with a shaking hand, "the roots of Yggdrasil..." Hiroshi nodded his head sagely and frowned. Tobias looked at Trollum and his face twisted into an annoyed expression. " Meaning?" Trollum looked at him incredulously.

"This is where Odin hung himself to gain the runes. This is where Ragnarok begins, this is where human magic started for the European world." Hiroshi coughed and stepped forward. "More so, it means we can't just break through. To do so would destroy everything that is tied to the worlds beyond this gate. Dwarves, elves, gnomes and western magic are just the beginning. Not to mention it would probably blow up Norway." Tobias spit on the ground and looked at the door crossly. "Then what do you suggest?" Trollums fingers traced the runes and a red spark of magic flashed within his eyes, "we open it."

A few hours later, Trollum had translated the runes and they were all listening to him speak inside the cargo hold of the plane. "It seems that the Nordic version of the fates never actually existed." He began as he looked at his notepad. "Essentially the three Norns, as mentioned in Snorri's stories, were three tests that determined a person's future. The first was a test of will power. The second was a test of internal strength. And, the final was a test against fear." The room was silent except for Bubba as he flicked his lighter open and lit another cigarette. "Alright, so what do these tests entail?"

Tobias said slowly as he leaned against the wall. "I have no clue," Trollum replied. He massaged the bridge of his nose and let out a sigh. "I do know though that once we go in there we aren't able to leave until the tests are been completed. Tobias stretched and cracked his knuckles, "ok well what are we waiting for? How do we get to Jormungdars pit afterward." A smile stretched across Trollums face and he held up the key, "actually we just put this in the right lock and then it tests us as we head there." Tobias nodded and looked at his friends, "I am going. If you don't want to come with me I won't think any less of you." Nobody said anything and Trollum smiled, " We are in this for the long run buddy." As they turned to leave Bubba called Tobias over, "listen I am going to stay with the plane as we planned. But I want you to have this." Bubba handed Tobias a small round object and the artic light glinted off a small metal pin. Tobias looked at it for a second and nodded, he knew what it was for.

Bubba's voice came from the radio on Tobias's hip as they stood looking at the giant keyhole on the door. "Alright, Y'all I am going to keep the plane idling and ready to go if you come out running." Tobias picked up the radio and spoke into it. "You know what to do if we aren't out by sunrise right?" Bubbas voice came out of the radio again, this time with a twinge of worry. "Take off and fly to Washington immediately. Alert the director of what has happened and then fly to California and find Cat and Akiri. Inform them that they need to petition the gods of every pantheon to intervene under the articles of alliance. Then find a hole and hide in it, I know. Hey, Tobias use what I gave you if you absolutely have to. " Tobias smiled and ignored the concerned glances from his friends, "Yeah man." "Good luck Y'all. I will be praying for ya." Bubba's voice came out from the radio and then it was silent. Tobias sighed and held the key up. His hands were shaking so badly he couldn't slide it in and he began to blush. Natalie's hand settled on his and slid the key home. "We can do this." She said as the world began to spin around them. "we have to." And then the world went black.

Tobias stared around them wide-eyed as lights began to shine in the darkness. Then he looked down and noticed that instead of snow he was standing on wood. The ground looked like bark and stretched out to either side of him for almost the length of half a football field. Above him, an interweaving tapestry of points of light and wood gleamed and below him stretched a long dark abyss. "Where the hell are we," He said out loud as everyone became accustomed to the new light. "Yggdrasil," Trollum said as he peered upwards, "the lowest branches it seems." Hiroshi let out a

muttered curse and stood up jerking his head from side to side. " It feels wrong, nothing like the immortal realms or the land of the Oni." Tom looked around in awe and nodded, "that's because you are Asian. This is European mythology. A different world entirely, you are probably the first kappa to ever set foot in this world." Hiroshi nodded and a grin spread across his face, "like Armstrong!"

Natalie let out a bark of laughter and grinned at them. "Let's move forward, I think the first test is probably somewhere along here." She stepped forward and Trollum stuck his hand out. "Hold on something is off." No sooner had the last syllable left his lips than a gate appeared at the other end of the branch. "So what now?" Tobias said as they all turned to look at the gate. Trollum shrugged, "who wants to do the test?" Hiroshi stepped forward and grinned darkly. Then he proceeded to take another step towards the door.

Like mist rising from a lake a figure materialized across the branch from him. It was a tengu dressed in a second world war imperial Japanese uniform. He had black feathers and was carrying a mass of white feathers in his hand which were dripping with blood. The specter was slightly see through but it was enough to make Hiroshi stop in his tracks. "??????????????" it said in a commanding voice. Hiroshi's hand moved towards his sword and began to wrap around the blade. Time seemed to stand still, and then his grip relaxed. "No," Hiroshi said calmly but with voice. Then he walked towards the specter. It started to stalk towards him slowly. Then in English, it said, "only a coward doesn't draw his sword." Hiroshi let out a steady breath and continued to move towards the door. The specter lunged at him with a roar and Hiroshi didn't even blink. A moment later his hand rested upon the door and his body sagged.

Everyone rushed forward and trollum placed a hand on Hiroshi's calf. "Are you ok?" he said as his friend shook. "No, but I will be" Hiroshi replied in a shaking voice. Then the gate swung open and showed a dark grey room made of stone in front of them. In the center of the room was a troll that towered over ten stories tall. Trollum gawked as the creature let out a mighty roar. Suddenly the world around them seemed to shimmer and change until they were all standing in the room together.

The mighty Troll let out another roar and flexed its muscles. Veins seemed to bulge from every inch of its rippling body and thick clear drool flowed from between its great tusks. In one hand it held a club made from the better part of an oak tree. In the other hand, it had a shield made from wood as well. With another bellow, it banged the club against its shield in a challenge. Tobias glanced and Trollum and grimaced. He was about to say they should draw straws when Tom stepped forward and looked at the troll with an appraising eye. "I can handle it," he said calmly as he slipped out of his armor. He was wearing tan pants and a white shirt with suspenders, he slipped out of the white shirt. Tobias looked at him in shock and placed a hand on the faries shoulder, "are you nuts?!" Tom smiled and brushed his friend's hand away, "I'm a Leprechaun." Then he marched towards the Troll wearing only a wife beater and tan pants and suspenders.

The troll stared down as the leprechaun approached it and grinned as it said, "MEAT". Tom wiped his nose on his arm and raised his fists, "right you are boyo. I am Thomas O'Neal Clancy. I am a friend to the Cait Sith and wielder of the coin of the north star. Prepare to die." The Troll let out a roar and swung its club in a sweeping motion towards Tom. Tom rolled to the left and leaped from the floor to the wall and then with supernatural strength and agility he landed on the club. His feet made a smacking sound as he ran along the club and towards the Trolls arm. The troll let out a bellow and swung his hand to smack Tom off of his club. Tom sneered and rolled forward but the hand still hit him and he fell from the club. But he didn't fall. Instead, Tom drew a small knife from his belt and sank it into the thigh of the troll.

Tom spit blood from the corner of his mouth and grinned at the group. Then with a scream, he threw himself upwards clawing his way up the body of the troll. The beast let out a terrified screech and tried to smack him away. But Tom dug his fingers in and used his teeth to bite through the creature's flesh and hold on. Finally, he made it to the top of the troll and drew his pistol from its holster. Then the troll began to shake its head violently until the gun tumbled from his blood slickened grasp. Tom spit out a curse and grimaced in anger. Then with a roar, the troll started towards his friend. Tom let out a roar of his own and with a burst of strength, he began to burrow into the Trolls eyeball. He used his hands and teeth to rip and tear at the flesh until with a scream the beast fell . Clawing at its eye, but it was already too late. Tom dug through the blood and ichor until he felt the creature fall still. Then he stood up and smiled.

Tobias and Trollum stared in horror and Hiroshi vomited. "WHAT THE HELL WAS THAT?!" Natalie screamed at Tom as he began to walk back towards them. "I won the test," Tom said defensively. Hiroshi finished throwing up and looked at him,

"HOW IS THAT INTERNAL STRENGTH TOM?!" Tom's smile grew and he shrugged, "being willing to be brutal if necessary?" Then with an audible pop, an open door appeared behind them. Through it drifted a familiar voice, "Hurry! Prepare the ritual to awaken the snake!" Mab's voice rang loud and clear and the group rushed towards the door.

As they entered the final test Tobias was struck by how simple it looked. It was a small room with a cloaked figure standing in front of a door. They all felt the world change around them but they didn't care, they were so close now. "So what now?" Tobias said as he took a step forward. Natalie shot her hand out and stopped him, "This is mine." she said as she shouldered her shotgun and walked towards the creature. As she approached the cloaked figures form seemed to change and melt. Then in almost the same amount of time, it takes to blink the Earlking stood in front of them.

"Hello my little plaything," the Erlking's voice seeped through the room and the figure smiled sickeningly. "Have you come for another game? Or maybe another chan-" Natalie slammed the but of her shotgun into the creatures face and sent it flying. "YOU THINK THIS SCARES ME?!" She screamed at the creature as it backed away from her blood streaming from its nose. The fake Earlking grinned and spit blood from its mouth. "I should I am going to ta-" Natalie smashed its face in with her boot heel (she had refused to wear heels). "You scared me once. You raped me and tortured me. You made me watch as my friend burned and then you took a future from me I didn't even know I could have had. Yes, I was afraid of you." She kicked him in the face again and he stared at her in shock. "Now you just piss me off." And with that Natalie kicked him until his jaw broke and hung open. Then she shoved the shotgun barrel between his teeth and grinned darkly. "You think you broke me with what you did but you are wrong. You made me stronger because I learned that there is nothing I can face that can take away who I am, a woman who is stronger than you will ever be." Then she pulled the trigger and the back of the fake Earlkings head exploded into a mist of blood and grey matter.

The door swung open and the room seemed to fall apart.

Tobias and his friends found themselves in a cave that seemed to stretch upwards forever. A few yards in front of them a cliff jutted out over an abyss. Tobias scanned the edge of the abyss and then he saw something that made his blood run cold. Frost was hanging in the air against one of the cavern walls. A blue light surrounded her and seemed to shimmer intermittently. Tobias let out a cry and started forward but was stopped as he felt two strong arms grab him from behind. His friends let out cries of alarm as they too were grabbed. Mab walked around from behind him to face him and grinned darkly. "Imagine my surprise when you appeared in the middle of my little ritual. Here I was chanting and planning to awaken the serpent with my daughter's blood and then you appear. And you even bring sacrifices!" Mab clapped her hands together and grinned, "Oh goody."

She leaned down and grinned at Trollum and then glanced at her guard, "are they all accounted for?" The guard shifted and nodded, "yes milady." Mab nodded and stood up, "A valiant attempt auditor but a foolish one. Tell me have you figured out the secret about my note?" She strolled over and began to examine each of his friends, making a tsking noise once she approached Natalie. "My dear it has been a while! What was it? Last Christmas when I told the Earlking he should teach you a lesson?" Natalie stared in shock at Mab and Tobias heard her breath catch. Mab's smile deepened and she stood up to walk back to Tobias, "The secret Tobias is that I lied on all but one of those verses. Someone will die." Then she turned back and motioned for Natalie's guard to step forward, "she will make an excellent sacrifice."

Tobias watched as Mab wrapped her hands around Natalie's throat and lifted her from the floor. "Stupid pitiful woman," Mab spit the words out like they were pieces of rotten fruit. She leaned up and sniffed Natalie's hair and grimaced. "I can still smell their touch on you girl. I can feel his stench radiating off of you in waves. I was there you know? Watching as they took you again and again. I encouraged them to do it, I watched them debase you until you were little more than an animal." Natalie began to cry as Mab began to drag her towards the edge of the cliff.

"I told them to do it in the first place. I told the Earlking to teach you a lesson about what humans mean to our kind. And he taught it to you didn't he? He took the one thing that made you a real woman and stripped it from you like clothing. I remember your screams." Mab lifted Natalie to her eye level and grinned evilly, "They were delectable." Natalie's tears came hard and fast and she struggled against Mab's grip. Mab's stare grew harder and her features became like ice. "And now you are going to die alone with nobody to save you. Now you will die with nothing but the memories that you are little more than a toy for creatures like me."

Tobias watched this exchange and he felt the heat building in his chest as his rage began to bloom. The guard tightened his grip until pain lanced through Tobias's arm and whispered, "Watch carefully maggot. Your friend is about to die." Tobias felt like he was going to burst rage built in his chest and then the dam holding it back began to crack and crumble. Then like a switch being flipped, it broke with a mighty internal snap of thunder. Tobias wriggled in the guard's arms and sank his teeth into the faries throat and jerked his head from side to side. Blood spurted from around his teeth and flowed down his face and neck. The guard let out a pained gurgle and fell to the ground as Tobias ripped his head back and spit out the larger part of the man's jugular. Tobias broke free of his arms and ran towards Mab screaming in an animal-like fury. He tackled her, wrenching her hands away from Natalie's throat. Forcing her to the ground Tobias screamed in rage and began to slam his fists into Mab's face again and again. Each blow was like hitting ice and did less and less damage and soon she was laughing at his pain. "Foolish human. You cannot harm a woman whose heart is made of ice." Tobias screamed in frustration and the room shook as jormungdar moved beneath them sensing his emotional state. He gazed at his friends and he saw the fear in their faces, his mind raced. He saw Natalie's tear-stained face he knew he knew what he had to do and that any moment Mab would overpower him and feed Natalie to the world serpent.

With a desperate burst of strength, Tobias grabbed Mab by the collar and stared into her eyes. "What are you doing?" Mab said, doubt seeping into her voice as she started to struggle. "I want you to see," Tobias said through gritted teeth and tears as he used all of his manic fueled strength and pulled her up to stand in front of him and his fury filled eyes. "I want you to see the soul of the man who kills you. I want you to see the soul of an IRS auditor." And with that, he let out a roar and grabbed Mab into a bear hug and dropped the grenade he had hidden in his hands. The same one that Bubba had given him on the plane. As it fell the sharp and unmistakable sound of a pin sliding from its casing sounded throughout the cavern The world stood still for a moment as Mab strained to get away from him in a wild panic. Her nails dug into his neck and chest and eyes, blood welled up thick and black where they struck his veins. Tobias counted the seconds before the grenade went off. On the last one, he tightened his grip and with a voice dripping with venomous hate whispered, "screw you ice bitch".

Trollum watched through tear-filled eyes as fire exploded from under his friend and engulfed the human and the fairy queen in a storm of fire and shrapnel. The icy cliff below them gave way before the force of the explosion and the two of them fell into the shadows of Jormungdar below. Trollum let out a scream and broke free of his captor. He ran to the edge of the ice screaming Tobias's name. Frost fell to the ground as the spell surrounding her dissipated and began to weep. Her piercing cry echoed off the cavern walls and the wind seemed to blow about her. Shards of ice flew from her in waves, never hurting her friends but shredding their captors. The group ran to the edge of the ice and stared into the black abyss. Tobias was gone and with him, the greatest threat humanity had known.

Or so they thought

"Wake up," a familiar voice said to Tobias. He hurt all over, even his fingertips were in pain. A boot tip nudged him until he opened his eyes and sat up and glared at a familiar face. Finally, he stood up and glowered at death as she grinned at him. "So I died?" he said as he looked around. He was standing on the sandy shores of a black river. It was cold but only enough to make him slightly uncomfortable. "Yeah," Death said in a slightly perkier tone than was necessary. "But I haven't taken you across yet." Tobias looked at her and shrugged, "why not?" Death's grin grew even bigger. "Tobias," she began. "Do you know why I hate being me?" Tobias shook his head and Death stopped grinning. "It is because people hate me. They think I am the end of everything. But there is so much more after death, an afterlife if you will." Death played with her hair and sighed, "But after a few hundred millennia you begin to wonder about life. What must it be like to feel, to love and to just be." Death gestured towards him and grinned again. "That's why I want to make a deal with you." Tobias looked at her in shock and could only nod as she continued.

"I want to have you give me one memory so I can know what life is like. In return, I will return you to life." Tobias looked at her in doubt. "Can I pick what the memory is?" She nodded and he thought about it for a second and then grinned. "I have the perfect one." Death walked towards him and he closed his eyes and began to remember. Tobias and Trollum laid on the ground moaning as Natalie stood up and smiled sweetly. "Tobias meet Trollum, you two get to be partners now. And in case you can't put two and two together special citizens means supernatural citizens." She leaned down right next to Tobias's ear and whispered, "Welcome to the IRS sweetheart. You should have taken the loans." At which point he fainted and his world was swallowed in an inky black sleep filled with dreams. Death gasped as she saw his dreams. Tobias walking around the IRS is a black suit. Tobias and Trollum eating lunch together and working on paperwork. Tears welled in her eyes as she saw that he had dreamed of having friends and a family. She started laughing when she saw how he had dreamed that maybe once, just once his life wouldn't be boring.

Death sighed as Tobias stopped remembering as she grinned silently. Then with a wave of her hand a phone appeared next to her and she picked it up. "I need the department of death and life ending. No not United Airways, the department next door to them... Hi Bob?" Tobias stared at her in shock as she began to speak in a more business-like tone. "I have a Tobias Schmit here but I don't have any paperwork for him." She winked at him and continued, "Yeah I know right? Freaking accounting must have counted out his years wrong. DO me a favor and make it so that he lives until he is well into his nineties. Yeah yeah, I will buy you a beer once you are off tonight." She said a few more things into the receiver and then hung up and sighed. She turned to look at him and seemed shocked, "Oh you are still here?" Then she shook her head and snapped her fingers. Black smoke swirled around him in a vortex and then he found himself behind his friends. And then he noticed something else, everything hurt like it was on fire. With a cry, Tobias fell to the ground and noticed that he was bleeding from claw marks and bite marks everywhere. He began to black out from the pain and just as he lost consciousness he was acutely aware of someone placing an ice cold hand on his face and soft lips on his own.

Two weeks later Tobias walked into his office and sighed. On the wall across from him hung a large newspaper that read, "Earthquakes silenced and extreme winter weather ending." The date for the newspaper read 1/18/2020. He rubbed his neck, flinching as his hand passed over one of his multiple bandages. Then he hobbled over to his desk and sat down and began to work on some paperwork. Trollum walked into the office and his grin was almost as big as his whole face. "Tobias, what are you doing here?!" Tobias looked up at his friend and grinned, "I have work to do." Trollum grunted and rolled his eyes, "You have a wedding to get to" Tobias nodded, "true." Trollum let out a laugh and shook his head. "By the way, there is a gift for you under your desk. It is from the director for 'excellence in the field'." Tobias looked under the desk and smiled as he pulled out a sleek black suitcase. Its handle and body were made of a darkly dyed letter and the clasps were polished brass. "Tobias lets gooooo you are going to be late!" Trollum urged as he pulled his hat out from under his own desk. But Tobias wasn't listening, he was too busy staring at the gold letters on the case.

They read, "Tobias Schmit, Auditor for the Supernatural"

END

TOBIAS SCHMIT AUDITOR FOR THE SUPERNATURAL
"The second year : New Boss New Problems"

COMING MARCH 2020

Tobias rolled onto his side and coughed up blood as he stared at the bodies laying next to him. "Well it seems you have finally reached the end of the road." Someone said as a pair of black leather boots appeared in his vision. "Death," Tobias coughed up more blood and smiled sickly. "I figured you might be coming around." Lady death knelled down and took Tobias's face in her hands and stared at him with concern. "I like you Tobias, I am sorry this had to happen to you." Tobias looked from death to the bodies surrounding him. His eyes ran over their faces and he coughed up more blood as tears began to form in his eyes.

Death looked at Tobias and placed a hand on his cheek. "I am sorry Tobias... it is not your time." Tobias's head hit the ground hard as he watched death walk over to the still form on the ground. He tried to scream as she nudged the body until it rolled over. A small brown fedora rolled out from one of the bodies outstretched hands. Tobias could only watch in horror as Death raised her scythe high and brought the blade down into the body.

An almost involuntary scream ripped through Tobias's chest. It sounded louder than usual but it was quickly replaced with sobs as Tobias felt the tears run down his face and onto the ground. He let out one croaking sob, which almost formed itself into a word on its own.

"Trollum"

"The Modern Canterbury Tales"
the stories Chaucer rejected

release date: TBA 2020

Sir Evan leaned back and took a long sip from his beer. His impressive mustache dropped into the beer suds and came back up covered in foam. "Indeed mister Chaucer I have many the great tales." Geoffrey Chaucer looked at the obese knight and arched an eyebrow. His hand reached into one of his many pockets and pulled out a gold coin. He tossed it to the barmaid who caught it without looking. She brought over more beer and ale, her bosom bouncing attractively as she sat the pitchers down onto the well-worn wooden table.

Chaucer leaned back and smiled as Sir Evan began to refill his glass. "I am only interested in one good sir knight." Sir Evan grinned and swayed slightly as drunk men are want to do. "What can you tell me about Robin of Loxley?" Sir Evan straightened up immediately and smiled, "You mean Robin Hood."

FABULOUSLY BROKEN!
A Southern Coming of Age Story

Release date: TBA 2021 (or earlier)

"DO NOT LISTEN TO THE DEVILS MUSIC CHILDREN!" Screamed the preacher one fine Sunday morning. It was your typical summer Sunday morning in the south. The birds were singing and the dogwood was in bloom. And a preacher was screaming about hellfire and damnation to a congregation with a combined IQ of about 16. Of course this was only if you discounted Benjamin (Ben to his friends) who was an exceptionally intelligent young man of thirteen. "AND BEWARE THE HOMO-SEXUALS! THEY WILL SNATCH YOUR CHILDREN UP AN-" Ben thought about his friend Andrew and decided he had listened enough and shouted in a clear voice, "No they won't! But mister Johnson will and mister Peterson has done that too!" The congregation was stunned and the preacher sputtered in shock. "Benjamin get your ass down." His mother hissed, her blond hair frizzing with irritation and her pale skin flushed red. "Why?" Ben replied, irritated and with tears forming in his eyes. He couldn't believe everybody was refusing to address the truth.

"Because they are members of the church! We don't talk about them like that." Ben stared at his mother in shock and found himself getting angry. "JUST BECAUSE THEY ARE MEMBERS OF THE CHURCH DOESN'T MEAN THEY SHOULDN'T BE EXPOSED!"

And at that statement all hell broke loose.

INDEX

Species of creatures in the Tobias-verse

Fae : Creatures of magic and folklore. Extremely powerful and sometimes worshiped as gods. These magical beings include many sub-classes some are listed below.

                Pixies
                Trolls
                Goblins
                High Faries
                Fae Queens
                Fae Lords
                Fae Regents
                Cait Siths
                Farie Spirits
                Leprechauns
                Red caps
                Brownies
                Tinkerers
                Elfins
                Draconids
                Dragons

Elves : Magical otherworldly beings. Extremely tall and graceful and well versed in magic and the arts. Famed for their pointed ears and eyesight.

Dwarves : Magical beings evolved from maggots which fed on Ymir's corpse. Famed for creating weapons and for being extremely intelligent. Common misconceptions state that their women have beards.

Fables : Beings formed from the primordial collective human

consciousness. Essentially, if the human race believes in a story enough then those characters come to life. Every fable has free will and is essentially immortal. But they have memories as if their stories really happened.... Maybe they really did?

Undead : Magical group of creatures who exist without the light of life or a soul. This group includes Vampires. These creatures also naturally repulse the living.

Cryptids : These creatures may be either supernatural or just weird. Their ranks include the Jersey Devil and Sasquatch. Cryptids are characterized as being very good at not being seen and as extremely intelligent creatures.

Cursed: This class of creature includes beings which have been cursed. This class includes werewolves and werepigs.

Aliens : Visitors from outer space.

Humans : People like you and me. The worst monsters of all.

Elementals : Spirits of the elements who manifest as humanoid shapes made out of their selected elements.

Gods : Ancient beings of immense powers who used to be (and in some cases still are) worshiped by humans and other creatures.

Divine creatures : Any creature that serves a god or goddess. Includes Angels, Demons, Valkyrie and Yokai.

Damned : Souls and creatures that were so evil in life that they are now confined to eternal torment. Or to work as lawyers and accountants.

Immortals : Humans who screwed around with magic and got made immortal. They are almost always morose and hate their lives.

Includes people like The Wandering Jew and John Dee.

Wizards/Witches : Humans who went to a school for magic and earned a degree.

Magi : The home schooled and shittier version of Wizards and witches

Warlocks : Wizards/Witches who have turned to darkness.

COMD : Creatures of Mass Destruction, these beings wield massive world destroying power. Some can even end reality as we know it. These include things like. Jourungdar. Fenrir, Jotun, The Beast, The Leviathan and The Kraken.

COUO : Creatures of Unknown Origin, Beings and things which nobody knows exactly what they are. These include things like living statues and the Mannequins.

Spirits : The deceased. Any creature or being can become a spirit after death, if they refuse to move on.

Avatars : Beings which embody some factor of human life. Examples of this are The Avatar of Video games and The Avatar of Trans-Fat. The most powerful Avatars are The Avatar of Madness and The Avatar of Reason.

The Ancient Ones : Beings from the outer planes of reality. Their followers have long been in the darkness. They are the creatures of horror and nightmare. Chaos incarnate. To look upon them would result in instant madness.

Organizations of the Tobias-verse

The sacred order of Saint Moses the Black : An order of catholic monks based around Saint Moses the Black (whose tale was recorded by Palladius's Lausaic Histories, a copy of this tale may be found further in the Index) who hunt down and cull the dangerous entities of the supernatural. They were essentially the first auditors.

The society of the Golem : A Jewish order who are named after the Golem of Prague. They specialize in business transactions within the supernatural community. They are extremely well known for their skills in diplomacy and contract making. They host an excellent potluck once a month.

The Family of the Black Rose : A vampire family who rule over Las Vegas Nevada. Well known for their involvement in the building of Vegas. As well as their involvement in the widespread slaughter that exists between mafia families within the city. Also they are well known benefactors of the NRA and many charitable organizations.

The Thule Society : A secret Nazi organization which is involved heavily in the occult. They took over the Republican party in 2016, and were almost wiped out in 2019 by Tobias. Famous for counting Adolf Hitler among their ranks, and crossdressing.

The Illuminati : They don't officially exist. That is all.

The Wild Hunt : A group of 'trooping' faeries. Famous for hunting down innocent and unsuspecting people. As well as for inspiring Wagners famous opera (a copy of the related transcripts may be found farther in the index)

The Einjar : Norse warriors who dine in Valhalla. They await Ragnarok and the final battle. They are often times willing to go to battle anyways as they cannot actually die.

Yamamotos Sword : The Japanese's imperial families supernatural management branch. They were merged with the EU's 'Grimm-stine' in 2001.

The deadly order of Saint Catherine the Bloody : A order of nuns who kick ass and chew bubble gum. And they are all out of gum.

The IRS : Our boys with paperwork. Hoo-rah!

US Government : The laughing stock of the world, and the bogey man of the supernatural world.

Chickenfeathers school of Wizardry and Witchcraft : A school of magic that is currently dealing with accreditation issues.

Monster Hunters : Bounty hunting rednecks with big trucks and even bigger guns. They kill innocent and evil supernatural beings alike and sell their remains.

Primary characters

Tobias W. Schmit : The most boring man on earth, or so his file says. Tends to tlike the simple things in life and has a unhealthy fascination with paperwork.

Trollum E. : If dynamite gained sentience it wouldn't be as explosive as Trollum. He is violent and takes no shit. Is very respected in the supernatural community. Adopted by dwarves.

Natalie Smith : The auditor before Tobias. She retired following an incident with the Earlking and a dragon. She suffers from severe PTSD which she masks with a wall of irritation and anger. Doesn't talk to her family in Tennessee because she couldn't save her brothers from man eating fungi.

The Director : An order obsessed Shoggoth from the outer planes of reality. Actually a nice guy and an excellent cook. Is married to Martha Petterson. A elementary school teacher. Currently wanted by the police for mentally destroying an abusive father.

Tom Peercy : A leprechaun who is gay. He loves to make the uniforms for the IRS auditors and to spend time with Dave.

Frost : Princess of the Fae Kingdom and Tobias's girlfriend. May or may not be pregnant as of new years.

Hiroshi : A kappa and an accountant who works with the IRS. A very skilled healer and spy.

Akiri : A Tengu and an Avian Vet. Very skilled in assassination and sword play.

Rapunzel : A princess and Trollums girlfriend. Loves punk rock and books.once kicked prince charming in the balls while screaming, "Down with the patriarchy!"

Royal families of the Tobias-verse

Fairy Royalty
Established: Fall of Ymir the Jotun
Head: Mab Queen of Darkness and Ice
Heir: Frost

Elvish Royalty
Established: The merging of Alfhime with the Norse world.
Head: Prince Regent
Heir: Sarah (due 2/13/2020)

Dwarvish Royalty
Established: After receiving titles from Odin and Tyr
Head: Malkak Granite Beard
Heir: Sutyr Granite Beard (or a suitable Jarl)

Hellish Monarchy
Established: During Lucifers fall
Head: Lucifer
Heir: Tiffany

Greek Gods
Established: Death of Kronos
Head: Zeus
Heir: Herakles

Norse Gods
Established: When they were licked out of Ice by a magic space cow
Head: Odin
Heir: Thor

Celtic Gods
Established: When the Dagda first touched soil
Head: Dagda
Heir: Morrigana

Chinese Gods
Established: The first Dynasty
Head:
Heir:

Indian Gods
Established: When Ganesh lost his head
Head: Kali
Heir: Ganesh

Japanese Spirits
Established: The first Japanese emperor
Head: The Oni consulate
Heir: Akamoro the Oni

Vampire Courts
Established: Transylvania 234 A.D
Head: Vlad Tempest
Heir: Vlad Dracul

Story of Saint Moses the Black (the first Auditor)
(as taken form the works of Palladius dated 348 A.D)

A certain Moses----this was his name----an Ethiopian by race and black, was house-servant to a government official. His own master drove him out because of his immorality and brigandage. For he was said to go even the length of murder. I am compelled to tell his wicked acts in order to show the virtue of his repentance. Anyhow they used to say that he was leader of a robber-band, and among his acts of brigandage one stood out specially, that once he plotted vengeance against a shepherd who had one night with his dogs impeded him in a project. Desirous to kill him, he looked about to find the place where the shepherd kept his sheep. And he was informed that it was on the opposite bank of the Nile. And, since the river was in flood and about a mile in extent, he grasped his sword in his mouth and put his shirt on his head and so got over, swimming the river. While he was swimming over, the shepherd was able to escape him by burying himself in the sand. So, having killed the four best rams and tied them together with a cord, he swam back again. [3] And having come to a little homestead he flayed the sheep, and having eaten the best of the flesh and sold the skins in exchange for wine, he drank a quart, that is eighteen Italian pints, and went off fifty miles further to where he had his band.

In the end this abandoned man, conscience-stricken as a result of one of his adventures, gave himself up to a monastery and to such practising of asceticism that he brought publicly to the knowledge of Christ even his accomplice in crime from his youth, the demon (a literal demon) who had sinned with him. Among other tales this is told of him. One day trolls attacked him as he sat in his cell, not knowing who it was. They were four in number. He tied them all together and, putting them on his back like a truss of straw, brought them to the church of the brethren, saying: "Since I am not allowed to hurt anyone, what do you bid me do with these?" Then these trolls, having confessed their sins and recognized that it was Moses the erstwhile renowned and far-famed destroyer of magic and evil, themselves also glorified God and renounced the world because of his power, saying to themselves: "If he who was is great and powerful in strength has feared God, why should we defer our salvation?"

This Moses was attacked by demons and spirits, who tried to plunge him into his old habit of sexual incontinence and crime. He instead waged a holy war upon them with sword and axe. He became known as the destroyer of Hell's armies and the Sin Eater. His titles numbered in the thousands as he laid waste upon the legions of the dammned. However he was tempted so greatly, as he himself testified, that he almost relinquished his purpose. So, having come to the great Isidore, the one who lived in Scete, he told him about his conflict.

And he said to him: "Do not be grieved. These are the beginnings of great things, and therefore they have attacked you the more vehemently, seeking out your old habit. For just as a dog in a butcher's shop owing to his habits cannot tear himself away, but if the shop is closed and no one gives him anything, he no longer comes near it. So also with you; if you endure, the demon gets discouraged and has to leave you." So he returned and from that hour practised asceticism more vehemently, and especially refrained from food, taking nothing except dry bread to the extent of twelve ounces, accomplishing a great deal of work and completing fifty prayers (a day). Thus he mortified his body, but he still continued to burn and be troubled by dreams.

Again he went to another one of the saints and said to him: "What am I to do, seeing that the dreams of my soul darken my reason, by reason of my sinful habits?" He said to him: "Because you have not withdrawn your mind from imagining these things, that is why you endure this. Give yourself to watching and pray with fasting and you will quickly be delivered from them." Listening to this advice also he went away to his cell and gave his word that he would not sleep all night nor bend his knees. So he remained in his cell for six years and every night he stood in the middle of the cell praying and not closing his eyes. And he could not master the thing. So he suggested to himself yet another plan, and going out by night he would visit the cells of the older and more ascetic (monks), and taking their water-pots secretly would fill them with water. For they fetch their water from a distance, some from two miles off, some five miles, others half a mile. So one night the demon watched for him, having lost his patience, and as he stooped down at the well gave him a blow with a cudgel across the loins (being that he punched him in the balls) and intended to leave him (apparently) dead, with no hesitation Moses grabbed the demon and cracked his skull upon the well.

   So the next day a man came to draw water and found Moses and the demon lying there, and told the great Isidore, the priest of Scete. He therefore picked moses up and brought him to the church, and for a year he was so ill that with difficulty did his body and soul recover strength. So the great Isidore said to him: "Moses, stop struggling with the demons, and do not provoke them." But he said to him: "I will never cease until the appearance of the demons ceases." So he said to him: "In the name of Jesus Christ your dreams have ceased. Come to Communion then with confidence, for, that you should not boast of having overcome passion, this is why you have been oppressed, for your good." And he went away again to his cell. Afterwards when asked by Isidore, some two months later, he said that he no longer suffered anything. Indeed, he was counted worthy of such a gift (of power) over demons that he feared flies more than he feared demons. This was the manner of life of Moses the Ethiopian; he too was numbered among the great ones of the fathers. So he died in Scete seventy-five years old, having become a priest; and he left seventy disciples. And they spread across the earth to form the first societies for dealing with the supernatural.

Coffee Recipe

INGREDIENTS
French Roast Coffee Beans (fresh ground)
Filtered and purified water
Heavy cream
Two teaspoons of sugar
A pinch of cinnamon
A pinch of nutmeg
chilled coffee cup (in fridge)

1. place coffee grounds in french press
2. add cinnamon and nutmeg
3. boil water until roiling
4. pour water into french press
5. sit for ten minutes
6. take coffee cup from fridge
7. fill 1/3 of the cup with cream
8. add sugar and stir until dissolved
9. add coffee

About the author

Steven L. Stamm is an "internet famous" poet and writer. He is well known for writing multiple short stories as well as publishing the "Tobias Schmit, auditor for the supernatural". He is also known for his work as a political activist for causes including LGBTQ rights and safe access for reproductive services for women. He has also invented multiple around the house objects including plans for a prototype bladeless garbage disposal. He has also mapped multiple miles of rural road in West Tennessee as part of a topographical hobby. As well as developing maps based on myth and legend to explain the potential geography of mythological worlds such as the Egyptian and greek afterlives. Mister Stamm is also a certified cryptozoologist and the leading expert in the branch of urban cryptozoology. However, mister Stamms primary contributions lie in his ghostwriting of articles and studies in the realm of human sexuality and cultural sexuality studies. He is also the developer of the "total honesty and primal participation" theory in human sexuality.

Mister Stamm is married to Jana B. Stamm. A loving wife and fellow poet.

He has accomplished all of this before his twenty-fifth birthday.

STEVEN L. STAMM

*author, poet, researcher, inventor, composer, chef, topographer
collector, appraiser, cryptozoologist, intercultural sexual studies
researcher, mythology researcher
intercultural communications scholar/researcher and activist*

Printed in Great Britain
by Amazon